LAIS

MARIE DE FRANCE

translated by
EUGENE MASON

Introduction

The tales included in this little book of translations are derived mainly from the "Lays" of Marie de France. I do not profess them to be a complete collection of her stories in verse. The ascription varies. Poems which were included in her work but yesterday are withdrawn today, and new matter suggested by scholars to take the place of the old. I believe it to be, however, a far fuller version of Marie's "Lays" than has yet appeared, to my knowledge, in English. Marie's poems are concerned chiefly with love. This, then, may be regarded as a volume of French romances, dealing, generally, with one aspect of medieval life.

An age so feminist in its sympathies as ours should be attracted the more easily to Marie de France, because she was both an artist and a woman. To deliver oneself through any medium is always difficult. For a woman of the Middle Ages to express herself publicly by any means whatever was almost impossible. A great lady, a great Saint or church-woman, might do so very occasionally. But the individuality of the ordinary wife was merged in that of her husband, and for one Abbess of Shrewsbury or Whitby, for one St. Clare or St. Hilda, there were how many thousand obscure sisters, who were buried in the daily routine of a life hidden with Christ in God! Doubtless the artistic temperament burst out now and again in woman, and would take no denial. It blew where it listed, appearing in the most unexpected places. A young nun in a Saxon convent, for instance, would write little dramas in Latin for the amusement and edification of the noble maidens under her charge. These comedies, written in the days of the Emperor Otho, can be read with pleasure in the reign of King George, by those who find fragrant the perfumes of the past. They deal with the pious legends of the Saints, and are regarded with wistful admiration by the most modern of Parisian playwrights. In their combination of audacity and simplicity they could only be performed by Saxon religious in the times of Otho, or by marionettes in the more self-conscious life of today. Or, again, an Abbess, the protagonist of one of the great love stories of the world, by sheer force of personality, would compose letters to one—how immeasurably her moral inferior, in spite of his genius—expressing with an unexampled poignancy the most passionate emotions of the heart. Or, to take my third illustration, here are a woman's poems written in an age when literature was almost entirely in the hands of men. Consider the strength of character which alone induced these three ladies to stray from the beaten paths of their sex. To the average woman it was enough to be an object of art herself, or to be the inspiration of masterpieces by man. But these three women of the Middle Ages—and such as they—

shunned the easier way, and, in their several spheres, were by deliberate effort, self-conscious artists.

The place and date of birth of Marie de France are unknown—indeed the very century in which she lived has been a matter of dispute. Her poems are written in the French of northern France; but that does not prove her necessarily to be a Frenchwoman. French was the tongue of the English Court, and many Englishmen have written in the same language. Indeed, it is a very excellent vehicle for expression. Occasionally, Marie would insert English words in her French text, the better to convey her meaning; but it does not follow therefrom that the romances were composed in England. It seems strange that so few positive indications of her race and home are given in her poems—nothing is contained beyond her Christian name and the bare statement that she was of France. She took great pride in her work, which she wrought to the best of her ability, and was extremely jealous of that bubble-reputation. Yet whilst this work was an excellent piece of self-portraiture, it reveals not one single fact or date on which to go. A consensus of critical opinion presumes that Marie was a subject of the English Crown, born in an ancient town called Pitre, some three miles above Rouen, in the Duchy of Normandy. This speculation is based largely on the unwonted topographical accuracy of her description of Pitre, given in "The Lay of the Two Lovers." Such evidence, perhaps, is insufficient to obtain a judgment in a Court of Law. The date when Marie lived was long a matter of dispute. The Prologue to her "Lays" contains a dedication to some unnamed King; whilst her "Fables" is dedicated to a certain Count William. These facts prove her to have been a person of position and repute. The King was long supposed to be Henry the Third of England, and this would suggest that she lived in the thirteenth century. An early scholar, the Abbé de La Rue, in fact, said that this was "undoubtedly" the case, giving cogent reasons in support of his contention. But modern scholarship, in the person of Gaston Paris, has decided that the King was Henry the Second, of pious memory; the Count, William Longsword, Earl of Salisbury, his natural son by Fair Rosamund; and that Marie must be placed in the second half of the twelfth century. This shows that scholarship is not an exact science, and that such words as "doubtless" should not be employed more than necessary. A certain Eastern philosopher, when engaged in instructing the youth of his country, used always to conclude his lectures with the unvarying formula, "But, gentlemen, all that I have told you is probably wrong." This sage was a wise man (not always the same thing), and his example should be had in remembrance. It seems possible (and one hesitates to use a stronger word) that the "Lays" of Marie were actually written at the Court of Henry of England. From political ambition the King was married to Eleanor of Aquitaine, a lady of literary tastes, who came from a family in which the patronage of singers was a tradition. Her husband, too, had a pronounced liking for literature. He was fond of books, and once paid a visit to Glastonbury to visit King Arthur's tomb. These, perhaps, are limited virtues, but Henry the Second had need of every rag. It is somewhat difficult to recognise in that King of the Prologue, "in whose heart all gracious things are rooted," the actual King who murdered Becket; who turned over picture-books at Mass, and never confessed or communicated. It is yet more difficult to perceive "joy as his handmaid" who, because of the loss of a favourite city, threatened to revenge himself on God, by robbing Him of that thing—i.e., the soul—He desired most in him; and whose very last words were an echo of Job's curse upon the day that he was born. Marie's phrases may be regarded, perhaps, as a courtly flourish, rather than as conveying truth with mathematical precision. If not, we should be driven to suggest an alternative to the favourite simile of lying like an epitaph. But I think it unlikely that Marie suffered with a morbidly sensitive conscience. There is little enough real devotion to be met with in her "Lays"; and if her last book—a translation from the Latin of the Purgatory of St. Patrick—is on a subject she avoids in her earlier work, it was written under the influence of some high prelate, and may be regarded as a sign that she watched the shadows cast by the western sun lengthening on the grass.

Gaston Paris suggests 1175 as an approximate date for the composition of the "Lays" of Marie de France. Their success was immediate and unequivocal, as indeed was to be expected in the case of a lady situated so fortunately at Court. We have proof of this in the testimony of Denis Pyramus, the author who wrote a Life of St. Edmund the King, early in the following century. He says, in that poem, "And also Dame Marie, who turned into rhyme and made verses of 'Lays' which are not in the least true. For these she is much praised, and her rhyme is loved everywhere; for counts, barons, and knights greatly admire it, and hold it dear. And they love her writing so much, and take such pleasure in it, that they have it read, and often copied. These Lays are wont to please ladies, who listen to them with delight, for they are after their own hearts." It is no wonder that the lords and ladies of her century were so enthralled by Marie's romances, for her success was thoroughly well deserved. Even after seven hundred years her colours remain surprisingly vivid, and if the tapestry is now a little worn and faded in places, we still follow with interest the movements of the figures wrought so graciously upon the arras. Of course her stories are not original; but was any plot original at any period of the earth's history? This is not only an old, but an iterative world. The source of Marie's inspiration is perfectly clear, for she states it emphatically in quite a number of her Lays. This adventure chanced in Brittany, and in remembrance thereof the Bretons made a Lay, which I heard sung by the minstrel to the music of his rote. Marie's part consisted in reshaping this ancient material in her own rhythmic and coloured words. Scholars tell us that the essence of her stories is of Celtic rather than of Breton origin. It may be so; though to the lay mind this is not a matter of great importance one way or the other; but it seems better to accept a person's definite statement until it is proved to be false. The Breton or Celtic imagination had peculiar qualities of dreaminess, and magic and mystery. Marie's mind was not cast in a precisely similar mould. Occasionally she is successful enough; but generally she gives the effect of building with a substance the significance of which she does not completely realise. She may be likened to a child playing with symbols which, in the hand of the enchanter, would be of tremendous import. Her treatment of Isoude, for example, in "The Lay of the Honeysuckle," is quite perfect in tone, and, indeed, is a little masterpiece in its own fashion. But her sketch of Guenevere in "The Lay of Sir Launfal" is of a character that one does not recall with pleasure. To see how Arthur's Queen might be treated, we have but to turn to the pages of a contemporary, and learn from Chrestien de Troyes' "Knight of the Cart," how an even more considerable poet than Marie could deal with a Celtic legend. The fact is that Marie's romances derive farther back than any Breton or Celtic dream. They were so old that they had blown like thistledown about the four quarters of the world. Her princesses came really neither from Wales nor Brittany. They were of that stuff from which romance is shaped. "Her face was bright as the day of union; her hair dark as the night of separation; and her mouth was magical as Solomon's seal." You can parallel her "Lays" from folklore, from classical story and antiquity. Father and son fight together unwittingly in "The Lay of Milon"; but Rustum had striven with Sohrab long before in far Persia, and Cuchulain with his child in Ireland. Such stories are common property. The writer takes his own where he finds it. Marie is none the less admirable because her stories were narrated by the first man in Eden; neither are Boccaccio and the Countess D'Aulnoy blameworthy since they told again what she already had related so well. Marie, indeed, was an admirable narrator. That was one of her shining virtues. As a piece of artful tale telling, a specimen of the craft of keeping a situation in suspense, the arrival of the lady before Arthur's Court, in "The Lay of Sir Launfal," requires a deal of beating. The justness and fineness of her sentiment in all that concerns the delicacies of the human heart are also remarkable. But her true business was that of the storyteller. In that trade she was almost unapproachable in her day. There may have been—indeed, there was—a more considerable poet living; but a more excellent writer of romances, than the author of "Eliduc," it would have been difficult to find.

The ladies who found the "Lays" of Marie after their own hearts were not only admirers of beautiful stories; they had the delicate privilege also of admiring themselves in their habit as they lived—perhaps even lovelier than in reality—amidst their accustomed surroundings. The pleasure of a modern reader in such tales as these is enhanced by the light they throw on the household arrangements and customs of the gentlefolk of the twelfth and thirteenth centuries. It may be of interest to consider some of these domestic arrangements, as illustrated by stories included in the present volume.

The corporate life of a medieval household centered in the hall. It was office and dining and billiard room, and was common to gentle and simple alike. The hall was by far the largest room in the house. It was lighted by windows, and warmed by an open fire of logs. The smoke drifted about the roof, escaping finally by the simple means of a lantern placed immediately above the hearth. A beaten floor was covered by rushes and fresh hay, or with rugs in that part affected by the more important members of the household. The lord himself and his wife sat in chairs upon a raised dais. The retainers were seated on benches around the wall, and before them was spread the dining table—a mere board upon trestles—which was removed when once the meal was done. After supper, chess and draughts were played, or minstrels sang ballads and the guest contributed to the general entertainment by the recital of such jests and adventures as commended themselves to his taste. If the hall may be considered as the dining room of the medieval home, the garden might almost be looked upon as the drawing room. You would probably get more real privacy in the garden than in any other part of the crowded castle, including the lady's chamber. It is no wonder that we read of Guenevere taking Launfal aside for a little private conversation in her pleasaunce. It was not only the most private, but also the most delightful room in the house—ceiled with blue and carpeted with green. The garden was laid out elaborately with a perron and many raised seats. Trees stood about the lawn in tubs, and there was generally a fountain playing in the centre, or possibly a pond, stocked with fish. Fruit trees and flower beds grew thickly about the garden, and a pleasanter place of perfume and colour and shade it would be difficult to imagine in the summer heat. The third room of which we hear continually in these romances is the lady's chamber. It served the purpose of a boudoir as well as that of a sleeping room, and consequently had little real privacy. It contained the marriage chest with its store of linen, and also the bed. This bed recurs eternally in medieval tales. It was used as a seat during the day, and as a resting-place of nights. It was a magnificent erection, carved and gilded, and inlaid with ivory. Upon it was placed a mattress of feathers, and a soft pillow. The sheets were of linen or silk, and over all was spread a coverlet of some precious material. An excellent description of such a couch is given in "The Lay of Gugemar." This chamber served also as a bath room, and there the bath was taken, piping hot, in the strange vessel, fashioned somewhat like a churn, that we see in pictures of the Middle Ages.

Of the dress of the ladies who moved about the castle, seeing themselves reflected from Marie's pages as in a polished mirror, I am not competent to speak. The type of beauty preferred by the old romancers was that of a child's princess of fairy tale—blue-eyed, golden-haired, and ruddy of cheek. The lady would wear a shift of linen, "white as meadow flower." Over this was worn a garment of fur or silk, according to the season; and, above all, a vividly coloured gown, all in one line from neck to feet, shapen closely to the figure, or else the more loosely fitting bliaut. Her girdle clipped her closely about the waist, falling to the hem of her skirt, and her feet were shod in soundless shoes, without heels. The hair was arranged in two long braids, brought forward over her shoulders; as worn by those smiling Queens wrought upon the western porch of Chartres Cathedral. Out of doors, and, indeed, frequently within, as may be proved by a reference to "The Lay of the Ash Tree," the lady was clad in a mantle and a hood. It must have taken a great deal of time and travail to appear so dainty a production. But to become poetry for others, it is necessary for a woman first to be prose to herself.

I am afraid the raw material of this radiant divinity had much to endure before she suffered her sea change. In medieval illustrations we see the maiden sitting demurely in company, with downcast eyes, and hands folded modestly in her lap. This unnatural restraint was induced by the lavish compulsion of the rod. If there was one text, above all others, approved and acted upon by fathers and mothers of the Middle Ages, it was that exhorting parents not to cocker their child, neither to wink at his follies, but to beat him on the sides with a stick. Turn to "The Lay of the Thorn," and mark the gusto with which a mother disciplines her maid. Parents trained their children with blows. Husbands (ah, the audacity of the medieval husband) scattered the like seeds of kindness on their wives. In a book written for the edification of his unmarried daughters, Chaucer's contemporary, the Knight of La Tour Landry, tells the following interesting anecdote. A man had a scolding wife, who railed ungovernably upon him before strangers, "and he that was angry of her governance smote her with his first down to the earth; and then with his foot he struck her on the visage, and broke her nose; and all her life after that she had her nose crooked, the which shent and disfigured her visage after, that she might not for shame show her visage, it was so foul blemished. And this she had for her evil and great language that she was wont to say to her husband. And therefore the wife ought to suffer, and let the husband have the words, and to be master." May I give yet another illustration before we pass from the subject. This time it is taken not from a French knight, but from a sermon of the great Italian preacher, St. Bernardino of Siena. "There are men who can bear more patiently with a hen that lays a fresh egg every day than with their own wives; and sometimes when the hen breaks a pipkin or a cup he will spare it a beating, simply for love of the fresh egg which he is unwilling to lose. Oh, raving madmen! who cannot bear a word from their own wives, though they bear them such fair fruit; but when the woman speaks a word more than they like, then they catch up a stick, and begin to cudgel her; while the hen that cackles all day, and gives you no rest, you take patience with her for the sake of her miserable egg—and sometimes she will break more in your house than she herself is worth, yet you bear it in patience for the egg's sake. Many fidgetty fellows, who sometimes see their wives turn out less neat and dainty than they would like, smite them forthwith; and meanwhile the hen may make a mess on the table, and you suffer her. Have patience; it is not right to beat your wife for every cause, no!"

At the commencement of this Introduction I stated that Marie's romances are concerned mainly with love. Her talent was not very wide nor rich, and I have no doubt that there were facets of her personality which she was unable to get upon paper. The prettiest girl in the world can only give what she has to give. By the time any reader reaches the end of this volume he will be assured that the stories are stories of love. Probably he will have noticed also that, in many cases, the lady who inspires the most delicate of sentiments is, incidentally, a married woman. He may ask why this was so; and in answer I propose to conclude my paper with a few observations upon the subject of medieval love.

I doubt in my own mind whether romance writers do not exaggerate what was certainly a characteristic of the Middle Ages. To be ordinary is to be uninteresting; and it is obvious that the stranger the experience, the more likely is it to attract the interest and attention of the hearer. Blessed is the person—as well as the country—who has no history. But it was really very difficult for the twelfth century poet to write a love story, with a maiden as the central figure. The noble maiden seldom had a love story. It is true enough that she was sometimes referred to in the choice of her husband. As a rule, however, her inclination was not permitted to stand in the way of the interests of her parents or guardians. She was betrothed in childhood, and married very young, for mercenary or political reasons, to a husband much older than herself. We read of a girl of twelve being married to a man of fifty. There was no great opportunity for a love story here; and the strange entreaty, on the part of the nameless French poet, to love the maidens for the sake of Christ's love, passed over the heads of the romance writers. Not that the medieval maidens showed any shrinking from matrimony. "Fair daughter, I have given you a husband." "Blessed be God," said the damsel. There spoke a contented spirit. Things have changed, and we can but sigh after the good old times.

But the maiden inevitably became the wife, and the whirligig of Time brought in his revenges. The lady now found herself the most important member of her sex, in a dwelling filled with men. She had few women about her person, and the confidant of a great dame in old romance is, frequently enough, her chamberlain. These young men had no chance of marriage, and naturally strove to gain the attention of a lady, whose favour was to them so important a matter. A medieval knight was the sworn champion of God and the ladies—but more especially the latter. The chatelaine, herself, found time hang heavily on her hands. Amusements were few;

books limited in number; a husband not of absorbing interest; so she turned to such distractions as presented themselves. The prettier a lady, the sweeter the incense and flattery swung beneath her nose; for this was one of the disadvantages of marrying an attractive woman. "It is hard to keep a wife whom everyone admires; and if no one admires her it is hard to have to live with her yourself." One of these distractions took the shape of Courts of Love, where the bored but literary chatelaine discussed delicate problems of conduct pertaining to the heart. The minstrel about the lady's castle, for his part, sought her favourable notice not only by his songs but also by giving an object lesson of his melancholy condition. One would imagine that his proceedings were not always calculated to further their purpose. A famous singer, for instance, in honour of a lady who was named Lupa, caused himself to be sewn in a wolf's skin, and ran before the hounds till he was pulled down, half dead. Another great minstrel and lover bought a leper's gown and bowl and clapper from some afflicted wretch. He mutilated his forefinger, and sat before his lady's door, in the company of a piteous crowd of sick and maimed, to await her alms. No doubt he trusted that his devotion would procure him a different kind of charity. From such discussions as these, and from conduct such as this, a type of love came into being which was peculiar to the period. Since the lovers were not bound in the sweet and common union of children and home, since on the side of the lady all was of grace and nought of debt, they searched out other bands to unite them together. These they found in a system of devotion, silence and faithfulness, which added a dignity to their relations.

The medieval romancer contemplated such unions with joy and pity; but for all their virtues we must not deceive ourselves with words. Such honour was rooted in dishonour, and the measure of their guilt was that they debased the moral currency. Presently the greatest of all the poets of the Middle Ages would arise, to teach a different fashion of devotion. His was a love that sought no communion with its object, neither speech nor embrace. It was sufficient for Dante to contemplate Beatrice from afar, as one might kneel before the picture of a saint. I do not say that a love like this—so spiritual and so aloof—will ever be possible to men. It did not suffice even to Dante, for all his tremendous moral muscle. Human love must always and inevitably be founded on a physical basis. But the burning drop of idealism that Dante contributed to the passion of the Middle Ages has made possible the love of which we now and again catch a glimpse in the union of select natures. And that the seed of such flowering may be carried about the world is one of the fairest hopes and possibilities of the human race.

The originals of these narratives are to be found in Roquefort's edition of the *Poésies de Marie de France.*

Eugene Mason

17

LAIS

PROLOGUE BY WAY OF DEDICATION

Those to whom God has given the gift of comely speech, should not hide their light beneath a bushel, but should willingly show it abroad. If a great truth is proclaimed in the ears of men, it brings forth fruit a hundredfold; but when the sweetness of the telling is praised of many, flowers mingle with the fruit upon the branch.

According to the witness of Priscian, it was the custom of ancient writers to express obscurely some portions of their books, so that those who came after might study with greater diligence to find the thought within their words. The philosophers knew this well, and were the more unwearied in labour, the more subtle in distinctions, so that the truth might make them free. They were persuaded that he who would keep himself unspotted from the world should search for knowledge, that he might understand. To set evil from me, and to put away my grief, I purposed to commence a book. I considered within myself what fair story in the Latin or Romance I could turn into the common tongue. But I found that all the stories had been written, and scarcely it seemed the worth my doing, what so many had already done. Then I called to mind those Lays I had so often heard. I doubted nothing—for well I know—that our fathers fashioned them, that men should bear in remembrance the deeds of those who have gone before. Many a one, on many a day, the minstrel has chanted to my ear. I would not that they should perish, forgotten, by the roadside. In my turn, therefore, I have made of them a song, rhymed as well as I am able, and often has their shaping kept me sleepless in my bed.

In your honour, most noble and courteous King, to whom joy is a handmaid, and in whose heart all gracious things are rooted, I have brought together these Lays, and told my tales in seemly rhyme. Ere they speak for me, let me speak with my own mouth, and say, "Sire, I offer you these verses. If you are pleased to receive them, the fairer happiness will be mine, and the more lightly I shall go all the days of my life. Do not deem that I think more highly of myself than I ought to think, since I presume to proffer this, my gift." Hearken now to the commencement of the matter.

The Lay of Gugemar

Hearken, oh gentles, to the words of Marie. When the minstrel tells his tale, let the folk about the fire heed him willingly. For his part the singer must be wary not to spoil good music with unseemly words. Listen, oh lordlings, to the words of Marie, for she pains herself grievously not to forget this thing. The craft is hard—then approve the more sweetly him who carols the tune. But this is the way of the world, that when a man or woman sings more tunably than his fellows, those about the fire fall upon him, pell-mell, for reason of their envy. They rehearse diligently the faults of his song, and steal away his praise with evil words. I will brand these folk as they deserve. They, and such as they, are like mad dogs—cowardly and felon—who traitorously bring to death men better than themselves. Now let the japer, and the smiler with his knife, do me what harm they may. Verily they are in their right to speak ill of me.

Hearken, oh gentles, to the tale I set before you, for thereof the Bretons already have made a Lay. I will not do it harm by many words, and here is the commencement of the matter. According to text and scripture, now I relate a certain adventure, which bechanced in the realm of Brittany, in days long gone before.

In that time when Arthur maintained his realm, the now in peace, the now in war, the King counted amongst his vassals a certain baron, named Oridial. This knight was lord of Leon, and was very near to his prince's heart, both in council chamber and in field. From his wife he had gotten two children, the one a son and the other a fair daughter. Nogent, he had called the damsel at the font, and the dansellon was named Gugemar—no goodlier might be found in any realm. His mother had set all her love upon the lad, and his father showed him every good that he was able. When the varlet was no more a child, Oridial sent him to the King, to be trained as a page in the courtesies of the Court. Right serviceable was he in his station, and meetly praised of all. The term of his service having come, and he being found of fitting years and knowledge, the King made him knight with his own hand, and armed him in rich harness, according to his wish. So Gugemar gave gifts to all those about his person, and bidding farewell, took leave, and departed from the Court. Gugemar went his way to Flanders, being desirous of advancement, for in that kingdom ever they have strife and war. Neither in Loraine nor Burgundy, Anjou nor Gascony, might be found in that day a better knight than he, no, nor one his peer. He had but one fault, since of love he took no care. There was neither dame nor maiden beneath the sky, however dainty and kind, to whom he gave thought or heed, though had he required her love of any damsel, very willingly would she have granted his desire. Many there were who prayed him for his love, but might have no kiss in return. So seeing that he refrained his heart in this fashion, men deemed him a strange man, and one fallen into a perilous case.

In the flower of his deeds the good knight returned to his own land, that he might see again his father and lord, his mother and his sister, even as he very tenderly desired. He lodged with them for the space of a long month, and at the end of that time had envy to hunt within the wood. The night being come, Gugemar summoned his prickers and his squires, and early in the morning rode within the forest. Great pleasure had Gugemar in the woodland, and much he delighted in the chase. A tall stag was presently started, and the hounds being uncoupled, all hastened in pursuit—the huntsmen before, and the good knight following after, winding upon his horn. Gugemar rode at a great pace after the quarry, a varlet riding beside, bearing his bow, his arrows and his spear. He followed so hotly that he over-passed the chase. Gazing about him he marked, within a thicket, a doe hiding with her fawn. Very white and wonderful was this beast, for she was without spot, and bore antlers upon her head. The hounds bayed about her, but might not pull her down. Gugemar bent his bow, and loosed a shaft at the quarry. He wounded the deer a little above the hoof, so that presently she fell upon her side. But the arrow glanced away, and returning upon itself, struck Gugemar in the thigh, so grievously, that straightway he fell from his horse upon the ground. Gugemar lay upon the grass, beside the deer which he had wounded to his hurt. He heard her sighs and groans, and perceived the bitterness of her pity. Then with mortal speech the doe spake to the wounded man in such fashion as this, "Alas, my sorrow, for now am I slain. But thou, Vassal, who hast done me this great wrong, do not think to hide from the vengeance of thy destiny. Never may surgeon and his medicine heal your hurt. Neither herb nor root nor potion can ever cure the wound within your flesh: For that there is no healing. The only balm to close that sore must be brought by a woman, who for her love will suffer such pain and sorrow as no woman in the world has endured before. And to the dolorous lady, dolorous knight. For your part you shall do and suffer so great things for her, that not a lover beneath the sun, or lovers who are dead, or lovers who yet shall have their day, but shall marvel at the tale. Now, go from hence, and let me die in peace."

Gugemar was wounded twice over—by the arrow, and by the words he was dismayed to hear. He considered within himself to what land he must go to find this healing for his hurt, for he was yet too young to die. He saw clearly, and told it to his heart, that there was no lady in his life to whom he could run for pity, and be made whole of his wound. He called his varlet before him,

"Friend," said he, "go forthwith, and bring my comrades to this place, for I have to speak with them."

The varlet went upon his errand, leaving his master sick with the heat and fever of his hurt. When he was gone, Gugemar tore the hem from his shirt, and bound it straitly about his wound. He climbed painfully upon the saddle, and departed without more ado, for he was with child to be gone before any could come to stay him from his purpose. A green path led through the deep forest to the plain, and his way across the plain brought him to a cliff, exceeding high, and to the sea. Gugemar looked upon the water, which was very still, for this fair harbourage was landlocked from the main. Upon this harbour lay one only vessel, bearing a rich pavilion of silk, daintily furnished both without and within, and well it seemed to Gugemar that he had seen this ship before. Beneath the sky was no ship so rich or precious, for there was not a sail but was spun of silk, and not a plank, from keel to mast, but showed of ebony. Too fair was the nave for mortal man, and Gugemar held it in sore displeasure. He marvelled greatly from what country it had come, and wondered long concerning this harbour, and the ship that lay therein. Gugemar got him down from his horse upon the shore, and with mighty pain and labour climbed within the ship. He trusted to find merchantmen and sailors therein, but there was none to guard, and none he saw. Now within the pavilion was a very rich bed, carved by cunning workmen in the days of King Solomon. This fair bed was wrought of cypress wood and white ivory, adorned with gold and gems most precious. Right sweet were the linen cloths upon the bed, and so soft the pillow, that he who lay thereon would sleep, were he sadder than any other in the world. The counterpane was of purple from the vats of Alexandria, and over all was set a right fair coverlet of cloth of gold. The pavilion was litten by two great waxen torches, placed in candlesticks of fine gold, decked with jewels worth a lord's ransom. So the wounded knight looked on ship and pavilion, bed and candle, and marvelled greatly. Gugemar sat him down upon the bed for a little, because of the anguish of his wound. After he had rested a space he got upon his feet, that he might quit the vessel, but he found that for him there was no return. A gentle wind had filled the sails, and already he was in the open sea. When Gugemar saw that he was far from land, he was very heavy and sorrowful. He knew not what to do, by reason of the mightiness of his hurt. But he must endure the adventure as best he was able; so he prayed to God to take him in His keeping, and in His good pleasure to bring him safe to port, and deliver him from the peril of death. Then climbing upon the couch, he laid his head upon the pillow, and slept as one dead, until, with vespers, the ship drew to that haven where he might find the healing for his hurt.

Gugemar had come to an ancient city, where the King of that realm held his court and state. This King was full of years, and was wedded to a dame of high degree. The lady was of tender age, passing fresh and fair, and sweet of speech to all. Therefore was the King jealous of his wife beyond all measure. Such is the wont of age, for much it fears that old and young cannot mate together, and that youth will turn to youth. This is the death in life of the old.

The castle of this ancient lord had a mighty keep. Beneath this tower was a right fair orchard, together with a close, shut in by a wall of green marble, very strong and high. This wall had one only gate, and the door was watched of warders, both night and day. On the other side of this garden was the sea, so that none might do his errand in the castle therefrom, save in a boat. To hold his dame in the greater surety, the King had built a bower within the wall; there was no fairer chamber beneath the sun. The first room was the Queen's chapel. Beyond this was the lady's bedchamber, painted all over with shapes and colours most wonderful to behold. On one wall might be seen Dame Venus, the goddess of Love, sweetly flushed as when she walked the water, lovely as life, teaching men how they should bear them in loyal service to their lady. On another wall, the goddess threw Ovid's book within a fire of coals. A scroll issuing from her lips proclaimed that those who read therein, and strove to ease them of their pains, would find from her neither service nor favour. In this chamber the lady was put in ward, and with her a certain maiden to hold her company. This damsel was her niece, since she was her sister's child, and there was great love betwixt the twain. When the Queen walked within the garden, or went abroad, this maiden was ever by her side, and came again with her to the house. Save this damsel, neither man nor woman entered in the bower, nor issued forth from out the wall. One only man possessed the key of the postern, an aged priest, very white and frail. This priest recited the service of God within the chapel, and served the Queen's plate and cup when she ate meat at table.

Now, on a day, the Queen had fallen asleep after meat, and on her awaking would walk a little in the garden. She called her companion to her, and the two went forth to be glad amongst the flowers. As they looked across the sea they marked a ship drawing near the land, rising and falling upon the waves. Very fearful was the Queen thereat, for the vessel came to anchorage, though there was no helmsman to direct her course. The dame's face became sanguine for dread, and she turned her about to flee, because of her exceeding fear. Her maiden, who was of more courage than she, stayed her mistress with many comforting words. For her part she was very desirous to know what this thing meant. She hastened to the shore, and laying aside her mantle, climbed within this wondrous vessel. Thereon she found no living soul, save only the knight sleeping fast within the pavilion. The damsel looked long upon the knight, for pale he was as wax, and well she deemed him dead. She returned forthwith to the Queen, and told her of this marvel, and of the good knight who was slain.

"Let us go together on the ship," replied the lady. "If he be dead we may give him fitting burial, and the priest shall pray meetly for his soul. Should he be yet alive perchance he will speak, and tell us of his case."

Without more tarrying the two damsels mounted on the ship, the lady before, and her maiden following after. When the Queen entered in the pavilion she stayed her feet before the bed, for joy and grief of what she saw. She might not refrain her eyes from gazing on the knight, for her heart was ravished with his beauty, and she sorrowed beyond measure, because of his grievous hurt. To herself she said, "In a bad hour cometh the goodly youth." She drew near the bed, and placing her hand upon his breast, found that the flesh was warm, and that the heart beat strongly in his side. Gugemar awoke at the touch, and saluted the dame as sweetly as he was able, for well he knew that he had come to a Christian land. The lady, full of thought, returned him his salutation right courteously, though the tears were yet in her eyes. Straightway she asked of him from what realm he came, and of what people, and in what war he had taken his hurt.

"Lady," answered Gugemar, "in no battle I received this wound. If it pleases you to hear my tale I will tell you the truth, and in nothing will I lie. I am a knight of Little Brittany. Yesterday I chased a wonderful white deer within the forest. The shaft with which I struck her to my hurt, returned again on me, and caused this wound upon my thigh, which may never be searched, nor made whole. For this wondrous Beast raised her plaint in a mortal tongue. She cursed me loudly, with many evil words, swearing that never might this sore be healed, save by one only damsel in the world, and her I know not where to find. When I heard my luckless fate I left the wood with what speed I might, and coming to a harbour, not far from thence, I lighted on this ship. For my sins I climbed therein. Then without oars or helm this boat ravished me from shore; so that I know not where I have come, nor what is the name of this city. Fair lady, for God's love, counsel me of your good grace, for I know not where to turn, nor how to govern the ship."

The lady made answer, "Fair sir, willingly shall I give you such good counsel as I may. This realm and city are the appanage of my husband. He is a right rich lord, of high lineage, but old and very full of years. Also he is jealous beyond all measure; therefore it is that I see you now. By reason of his jealousy he has shut me fast between high walls, entered by one narrow door, with an ancient priest to keep the key. May God requite him for his deed. Night and day I am guarded in this prison, from whence I may never go forth, without the knowledge of my lord. Here are my chamber and my chapel, and here I live, with this, my maiden, to bear me company. If it pleases you to dwell here for a little, till you may pass upon your way, right gladly we shall receive you, and with a good heart we will tend your wound, till you are healed."

When Gugemar heard this speech he rejoiced greatly. He thanked the lady with many sweet words, and consented to sojourn in her hall awhile. He raised himself upon his couch, and by the courtesy of the damsels left the ship. Leaning heavily upon the lady, at the end he won to her maiden's chamber, where there was a fair bed covered with a rich dossal of broidered silk, edged with fur. When he was entered in this bed, the damsels came bearing clear water in basins of gold, for the cleansing of his hurt. They stanched the blood with a towel of fine linen, and bound the wound strictly, to his exceeding comfort. So after the vesper meal was eaten, the lady departed to her own chamber, leaving the knight in much ease and content.

Now Gugemar set his love so fondly upon the lady that he forgot his father's house. He thought no more of the anguish of his hurt, because of another wound that was beneath his breast. He tossed and sighed in his unrest, and prayed the maiden of his service to depart, so that he might sleep a little. When the maid was gone, Gugemar considered within himself whether he might seek the dame, to know whether her heart was warmed by any ember of the flame that burned in his. He turned it this way and that, and knew not what to do. This only was clear, that if the lady refused to search his wound, death, for him, was sure and speedy.

"Alas," said he, "what shall I do! Shall I go to my lady, and pray her pity on the wretch who has none to give him counsel? If she refuse my prayer, because of her hardness and pride, I shall know there is nought for me but to die in my sorrow, or, at least, to go heavily all the days of my life."

Then he sighed, and in his sighing lighted on a better purpose; for he said within himself that doubtless he was born to suffer, and that the best of him was tears. All the long night he spent in vigil and groanings and watchfulness. To himself he told over her words and her semblance. He remembered the eyes and the fair mouth of his lady, and all the grace and the sweetness, which had struck like a knife at his heart. Between his teeth he cried on her for pity, and for a little more would have called her to his side. Ah, had he but known the fever of the lady, and how terrible a lord to her was Love, how great had been his joy and solace. His visage would have been the more sanguine, which was now so pale of colour, because of the dolour that was his. But if the knight was sick by reason of his love, the dame had small cause to boast herself of health. The lady rose early from her bed, since she might not sleep. She complained of her unrest, and of Love who rode her so hardly. The maiden, who was of her company, saw clearly enough that all her lady's thoughts were set upon the knight, who, for his healing, sojourned in the chamber. She did not know whether his thoughts were given again to the dame. When, therefore, the lady had entered in the chapel, the damsel went straightway to the knight. He welcomed her gladly, and bade her be seated near the bed. Then he inquired, "Friend, where now is my lady, and why did she rise so early from her bed?"

Having spoken so far, he became silent, and sighed.

"Sir," replied the maiden softly, "you love, and are discreet, but be not too discreet therein. In such a love as yours there is nothing to be ashamed. He who may win my lady's favour has every reason to be proud of his fortune. Altogether seemly would be your friendship, for you are young, and she is fair."

The knight made answer to the maiden, "I am so fast in the snare, that I pray the fowler to slay me, if she may not free me from the net. Counsel me, fair sweet friend, if I may hope of kindness at her hand."

Then the maiden of her sweetness comforted the knight, and assured him of all the good that she was able. So courteous and debonair was the maid.

When the lady had heard Mass, she hastened back to the chamber. She had not forgotten her friend, and greatly she desired to know whether he was awake or asleep, of whom her heart was fain. She bade her maiden to summon him to her chamber, for she had a certain thing in her heart to show him at leisure, were it for the joy or the sorrow of their days.

Gugemar saluted the lady, and the dame returned the knight his courtesy, but their hearts were too fearful for speech. The knight dared ask nothing of his lady, for reason that he was a stranger in a strange land, and was adread to show her his love. But—as says the proverb— he who will not tell of his sore, may not hope for balm to his hurt. Love is a privy wound within the heart, and none knoweth of that bitterness but the heart alone. Love is an evil which may last for a whole life long, because of man and his constant heart. Many there be who make of Love a gibe and a jest, and with specious words defame him by boastful tales. But theirs is not love. Rather it is folly and lightness, and the tune of a merry song. But let him who has found a constant lover prize her above rubies, and serve her with loyal service, being altogether at her will. Gugemar loved in this fashion, and therefore Love came swiftly to his aid. Love put words in his mouth, and courage in his heart, so that his hope might be made plain.

"Lady," said he, "I die for your love. I am in fever because of my wound, and if you care not to heal my hurt I would rather die. Fair friend, I pray you for grace. Do not gainsay me with evil words."

The lady hearkened with a smile to Gugemar's speech. Right daintily and sweetly she replied, "Friend, yea is not a word of two letters. I do not grant such a prayer every day of the week, and must you have your gift so quickly?"

"Lady," cried he, "for God's sake pity me, and take it not amiss. She, who loves lightly, may make her lover pray for long, so that she may hide how often her feet have trodden the pathway with another friend. But the honest dame, when she has once given her heart to a friend, will not deny his wish because of pride. The rather she will find her pride in humbleness, and love him again with the same love he has set on her. So they will be glad together, and since none will have knowledge or hearing of the matter, they will rejoice in their youth. Fair, sweet lady, be this thy pleasure?"

When the lady heard these words well she found them honest and true. Therefore without further prayings and ado she granted Gugemar her love and her kiss. Henceforward Gugemar lived greatly at his ease, for he had sight and speech of his friend, and many a time she granted him her embrace and tenderness, as is the wont of lovers when alone.

For a year and a half Gugemar dwelt with his lady, in solace and great delight. Then Fortune turned her wheel, and in a trice cast those down, whose seat had been so high. Thus it chanced to them, for they were spied upon and seen.

On a morning in summer time the Queen and the damoiseau sat fondly together. The knight embraced her, eyes and face, but the lady stayed him, saying, "Fair sweet friend, my heart tells me that I shall lose you soon, for this hidden thing will quickly be made clear. If you are slain, may the same sword kill me. But if you win forth, well I know that you will find another love, and that I shall be left alone with my thoughts. Were I parted from you, may God give me neither joy, nor rest, nor peace, if I would seek another friend. Of that you need have no fear. Friend, for surety and comfort of my heart deliver me now some sark of thine. Therein I will set a knot, and make this covenant with you, that never will you put your love on dame or maiden, save only on her who shall first unfasten this knot. Then you will ever keep faith with me, for so cunning shall be my craft, that no woman may hope to unravel that coil, either by force or guile, or even with her knife."

So the knight rendered the sark to his lady, and made such bargain as she wished, for the peace and assurance of her mind.

For his part the knight took a fair girdle, and girt it closely about the lady's middle. Right secret was the clasp and buckle of this girdle. Therefore he required of the dame that she would never grant her love, save to him only, who might free her from the strictness of this bond, without injury to band or clasp. Then they kissed together, and entered into such covenant as you have heard.

That very day their hidden love was made plain to men. A certain chamberlain was sent by that ancient lord with a message to the Queen. This unlucky wretch, finding that in no wise could he enter within the chamber, looked through the window, and saw. Forthwith he hastened to the King, and told him that which he had seen. When the agèd lord understood these words, never was there a sadder man than he. He called together the most trusty sergeants of his guard, and coming with them to the Queen's chamber, bade them to thrust in the door. When Gugemar was found therein, the King commanded that he should be slain with the sword, by reason of the anguish that was his. Gugemar was in no whit dismayed by the threat. He started to his feet, and gazing round, marked a stout rod of fir, on which it is the use for linen to be hung. This he took in hand, and faced his foes, bidding them have a care, for he would do a mischief to them all. The King looked earnestly upon the fearless knight, inquiring of him who he was, and where he was born, and in what manner he came to dwell within his house. So Gugemar told over to him this story of his fate. He showed him of the Beast that he had wounded to his hurt; of the nave, and of his bitter wound; of how he came within the realm, and of the lady's surgery. He told all to the ancient lord, to the last moment when he stood within his power. The King replied that he gave no credence to his word, nor believed that the story ran as he had said. If, however, the vessel might be found, he would commit the knight again to the waves. He would go the more heavily for the knight's saining, and a glad day would it be if he made shipwreck at sea. When they had entered into this covenant together, they went forth to the harbour, and there discovered the barge, even as Gugemar had said. So they set him thereon, and prayed him to return unto his own realm.

Without sail or oar the ship parted from that coast, with no further tarrying. The knight wept and wrung his hands, complaining of his lady's loss, and of her cherishing. He prayed the mighty God to grant him speedy death, and never to bring him home, save to meet again with her who was more desirable than life. Whilst he was yet at his orisons, the ship drew again to that port, from whence she had first come. Gugemar made haste to get him from the vessel, so that he might the more swiftly return to his own land. He had gone but a little way when he was aware of a squire of his household, riding in the company of a certain knight. This squire held the bridle of a destrier in his hand, though no man rode thereon. Gugemar called to him by name, so that the varlet looking upon him, knew again his lord. He got him to his feet, and bringing the destrier to his master, set the knight thereon. Great was the joy, and merry was the feast, when Gugemar returned to his own realm. But though his friends did all that they were able, neither song nor game could cheer the knight, nor turn him from dwelling in his unhappy thoughts. For peace of mind they urged that he took to himself a wife, but Gugemar would have none of their counsel. Never would he wed a wife, on any day, either for love or for wealth, save only that she might first unloose the knot within his shirt. When this news was noised about the country, there was neither dame nor damsel in the realm of Brittany, but essayed to unfasten the knot. But there was no lady who could gain to her wish, whether by force or guile.

Now will I show of that lady, whom Gugemar so fondly loved. By the counsel of a certain baron the ancient King set his wife in prison. She was shut fast in a tower of grey marble, where her days were bad, and her nights worse. No man could make clear to you the great pain, the anguish and the dolour, that she suffered in this tower, wherein, I protest, she died daily. Two years and more she lay bound in prison, where warders came, but never joy or delight. Often she thought upon her friend.

"Gugemar, dear lord, in an evil hour I saw you with my eyes. Better for me that I die quickly, than endure longer my evil lot. Fair friend, if I could but win to that coast whence you sailed, very swiftly would I fling myself in the sea, and end my wretched life." When she had said these words she rose to her feet, and coming to the door was amazed to find therein neither bolt nor key. She issued forth, without challenge from sergeant or warder, and hastening to the harbour, found there her lover's ship, made fast to that very rock, from which she would cast her down. When she saw the barge she climbed thereon, but presently bethought her that on this nave her friend had gone to perish in the sea. At this thought she would have fled again to the shore, but her bones were as water, and she fell upon the deck. So in sore travail and sorrow, the vessel carried her across the waves, to a port of Brittany, guarded by a castle, strong and very fair. Now the lord of this castle was named Meriadus. He was a right warlike prince, and had made him ready to fight with the prince of a country near by. He had risen very early in the morning, to send forth a great company of spears, the more easily to ravage this neighbour's realm. Meriadus looked forth from his window, and marked the ship which came to port. He hastened down the steps of the perron, and calling to his chamberlain, came with what speed he might to the nave. Then mounting the ladder he stood upon the deck. When Meriadus found within the ship a dame, who for beauty seemed rather a fay than a mere earthly woman, he seized her by her mantle, and brought her swiftly to his keep. Right joyous was he because of his good fortune, for lovely was the lady beyond mortal measure. He made no question as to who had set her on the barge. He knew only that she was fair, and of high lineage, and that his heart turned towards her with so hot a love as never before had he put on dame or damsel. Now there dwelt within the castle a sister of this lord, who was yet unwed. Meriadus bestowed the lady in his sister's chamber, because it was the fairest in the tower. Moreover he commanded that she should be meetly served, and held in all reverence. But though the dame was so richly clothed and cherished, ever was she sad and deep in thought. Meriadus came often to cheer her with mirth and speech, by reason that he wished to gain her love as a free gift, and not by force. It was in vain that he prayed her for grace, since she had no balm for his wound. For answer she showed him the girdle about her body, saying that never would she give her love to man, save only to him who might unloose the buckle of that girdle, without harm to belt or clasp. When Meriadus heard these words, he spoke in haste and said,

"Lady, there dwells in this country a very worthy knight, who will take no woman as wife, except she first untie a certain crafty knot in the hem of a shirt, and that without force or knife. For a little I would wager that it was you who tied this knot."

When the lady heard thereof her breath went from her, and near she came to falling on the ground. Meriadus caught her in his arms, and cut the laces of her bodice, that she might have the more air. He strove to unfasten her girdle, but might not dissever the clasp. Yea, though every knight in the realm essayed to unfasten that cincture, it would not yield, except to one alone.

Now Meriadus made the lists ready for a great jousting, and called to that tournament all the knights who would aid him in his war. Many a lord came at his bidding, and with them Gugemar, amongst the first. Meriadus had sent letters to the knight, beseeching him, as friend and companion, not to fail him in this business. So Gugemar hastened to the need of his lord, and at his back more than one hundred spears. All these Meriadus welcomed very gladly, and gave them lodging within his tower. In honour of his guest, the prince sent two gentlemen to his sister, praying her to attire herself richly, and come to hall, together with the dame whom he loved so dearly well. These did as they were bidden, and arrayed in their sweetest vesture, presently entered in the hall, holding each other by the hand. Very pale and pensive was the lady, but when she heard her lover's name her feet failed beneath her, and had not the maiden held her fast, she would have fallen on the floor. Gugemar rose from his seat at the sight of the dame, her fashion and her semblance, and stood staring upon her. He went a little apart, and said within himself, "Can this be my sweet friend, my hope, my heart, my life, the fair lady who gave me the grace of her love? From whence comes she; who might have brought her to this far land? But I speak in my folly, for well I know that this is not my dear. A little red, a little white, and all women are thus shapen. My thoughts are troubled, by reason that the sweetness of this lady resembles the sweetness of that other, for whom my heart sighs and trembles. Yet needs must that I have speech of the lady."

Gugemar drew near to the dame. He kissed her courteously, and found no word to utter, save to pray that he might be seated at her side. Meriadus spied upon them closely, and was the more heavy because of their trouble. Therefore he feigned mirth.

"Gugemar, dear lord, if it pleases you, let this damsel essay to untie the knot of your sark, if so be she may loosen the coil."

Gugemar made answer that very willingly he would do this thing. He called to him a squire who had the shirt in keeping, and bade him seek his charge, and deliver it to the dame. The lady took the sark in hand. Well she knew the knot that she had tied so cunningly, and was so willing to unloose; but for reason of the trouble at her heart, she did not dare essay. Meriadus marked the distress of the damsel, and was more sorrowful than ever was lover before.

"Lady," said he, "do all that you are able to unfasten this coil."

So at his commandment she took again to her the hem of the shirt, and lightly and easily unravelled the tie.

Gugemar marvelled greatly when he saw this thing. His heart told him that of a truth this was his lady, but he could not give faith to his eyes.

"Friend, are you indeed the sweet comrade I have known? Tell me truly now, is there about your body the girdle with which I girt you in your own realm?"

He set his hands to her waist, and found that the secret belt was yet about her sides.

"Fair sweet friend, tell me now by what adventure I find you here, and who has brought you to this tower?"

So the lady told over to her friend the pain and the anguish and the dolour of the prison in which she was held; of how it chanced that she fled from her dungeon, and lighting upon a ship, entered therein, and came to this fair haven; of how Meriadus took her from the barge, but kept her in all honour, save only that ever he sought for her love; "but now, fair friend, all is well, for you hold your lady in your arms."

Gugemar stood upon his feet, and beckoned with his hand.

"Lords," he cried, "hearken now to me. I have found my friend, whom I have lost for a great while. Before you all I pray and require of Meriadus to yield me my own. For this grace I give him open thanks. Moreover I will kneel down, and become his liege man. For two years, or three, if he will, I will bargain to serve in his quarrels, and with me, of riders, a hundred or more at my back."

Then answered Meriadus, "Gugemar, fair friend, I am not yet so shaken or overborne in war, that I must do as you wish, right humbly. This woman is my captive. I found her: I hold her: and I will defend my right against you and all your power."

When Gugemar heard these proud words he got to horse speedily, him and all his company. He threw down his glove, and parted in anger from the tower. But he went right heavily, since he must leave behind his friend. In his train rode all those knights who had drawn together to that town for the great tournament. Not a knight of them all but plighted faith to follow where he led, and to hold himself recreant and shamed if he failed his oath.

That same night the band came to the castle of the prince with whom Meriadus was at war. He welcomed them very gladly, and gave them lodging in his tower. By their aid he had good hope to bring this quarrel to an end. Very early in the morning the host came together to set the battle in array. With clash of mail and noise of horns they issued from the city gate, Gugemar riding at their head. They drew before the castle where Meriadus lay in strength, and sought to take it by storm. But the keep was very strong, and Meriadus bore himself as a stout and valiant knight. So Gugemar, like a wary captain, sat himself down before the town, till all the folk of that place were deemed by friend and sergeant to be weak with hunger. Then they took that high keep with the sword, and burnt it with fire. The lord thereof they slew in his own hall; but Gugemar came forth, after such labours as you have heard, bearing his lady with him, to return in peace to his own land.

From this adventure that I have told you, has come the Lay that minstrels chant to harp and viol—fair is that song and sweet the tune.

THE LAY OF THE DOLOROUS KNIGHT

Hearken now to the Lay that once I heard a minstrel chanting to his harp. In surety of its truth I will name the city where this story passed. The Lay of the Dolorous Knight, my harper called his song, but of those who hearkened, some named it rather, The Lay of the Four Sorrows.

In Nantes, of Brittany, there dwelt a dame who was dearly held of all, for reason of the much good that was found in her. This lady was passing fair of body, apt in book as any clerk, and meetly schooled in every grace that it becometh dame to have. So gracious of person was this damsel, that throughout the realm there was no knight could refrain from setting his heart upon her, though he saw her but one only time. Although the demoiselle might not return the love of so many, certainly she had no wish to slay them all. Better by far that a man pray and require in love all the dames of his country, than run mad in woods for the bright eyes of one. Therefore this dame gave courtesy and good will to each alike. Even when she might not hear a lover's words, so sweetly she denied his wish that the more he held her dear and was the more her servant for that fond denial. So because of her great riches of body and of heart, this lady of whom I tell, was prayed and required in love by the lords of her country, both by night and by day.

Now in Brittany lived four young barons, but their names I cannot tell. It is enough that they were desirable in the eyes of maidens for reason of their beauty, and that men esteemed them because they were courteous of manner and open of hand. Moreover they were stout and hardy knights amongst the spears, and rich and worthy gentlemen of those very parts. Each of these four knights had set his heart upon the lady, and for love of her pained himself mightily, and did all that he was able, so that by any means he might gain her favour. Each prayed her privily for her love, and strove all that he could to make him worthy of the gift, above his fellows. For her part the lady was sore perplexed, and considered in her mind very earnestly, which of these four knights she should take as friend. But since they all were loyal and worthy gentlemen, she durst not choose amongst them; for she would not slay three lovers with her hand so that one might have content. Therefore to each and all, the dame made herself fair and sweet of semblance. Gifts she gave to all alike. Tender messages she sent to each. Every knight deemed himself esteemed and favoured above his fellows, and by soft words and fair service diligently strove to please. When the knights gathered together for the games, each of these lords contended earnestly for the prize, so that he might be first, and draw on him the favour of his dame. Each held her for his friend. Each bore upon him her gift—pennon, or sleeve, or ring. Each cried her name within the lists.

Now when Eastertide was come, a great tournament was proclaimed to be held beyond the walls of Nantes, that rich city. The four lovers were the appellants in this tourney, and from every realm knights rode to break a lance in honour of their dame. Frenchman and Norman and Fleming; the hardiest knights of Brabant, Boulogne and Anjou; each came to do his devoir in the field. Nor was the chivalry of Nantes backward in this quarrel, but till the vespers of the tournament was come, they stayed themselves within the lists, and struck stoutly for their lord. After the four lovers had laced their harness upon them, they issued forth from the city, followed by the knights who were of their company in this adventure. But upon the four fell the burden of the day, for they were known of all by the embroidered arms upon their surcoat, and the device fashioned on the shield. Now against the four lovers arrayed themselves four other knights, armed altogether in coats of mail, and helmets and gauntlets of steel. Of these stranger knights two were of Hainault, and the two others were Flemings. When the four lovers saw their adversaries prepare themselves for the combat, they had little desire to flee, but hastened to join them in battle. Each lowered his spear, and choosing his enemy, met him so eagerly that all men wondered, for horse and man fell to the earth. The four lovers recked little of their destriers, but freeing their feet from the stirrups bent over the fallen foe, and called on him to yield. When the friends of the vanquished knights saw their case, they hastened to their succour; so for their rescue there was a great press, and many a mighty stroke with the sword.

The damsel stood upon a tower to watch these feats of arms. By their blazoned coats and shields she knew her knights; she saw their marvellous deeds, yet might not say who did best, nor give to one the praise. But the tournament was no longer a seemly and ordered battle. The ranks of the two companies were confused together, so that every man fought against his fellow, and none might tell whether he struck his comrade or his foe. The four lovers did well and worshipfully, so that all men deemed them worthy of the prize. But when evening was come, and the sport drew to its close, their courage led them to folly. Having ventured too far from their companions, they were set upon by their adversaries, and assailed so fiercely that three were slain outright. As to the fourth he yet lived, but altogether mauled and shaken, for his thigh was broken, and a spear head remained in his side. The four bodies were fallen on the field, and lay with those who had perished in that day. But because of the great mischief these four lovers had done their adversaries, their shields were cast despitefully without the lists; but in this their foemen did wrongfully, and all men held them in sore displeasure.

Great were the lamentation and the cry when the news of this mischance was noised about the city. Such a tumult of mourning was never before heard, for the whole city was moved. All men hastened forth to the place where the lists were set. Meetly to mourn the dead there rode nigh upon two thousand knights, with hauberks unlaced, and uncovered heads, plucking upon their beards. So the four lovers were placed each upon his shield, and being brought back in honour to Nantes, were carried to the house of that dame, whom so greatly they had loved. When the lady knew this distressful adventure, straightway she fell to the ground. Being returned from her swoon, she made her complaint, calling upon her lovers each by his name.

"Alas," said she, "what shall I do, for never shall I know happiness again. These four knights had set their hearts upon me, and despite their great treasure, esteemed my love as richer than all their wealth. Alas, for the fair and valiant knight! Alas, for the loyal and generous man! By gifts such as these they sought to gain my favour, but how might lady bereave three of life, so as to cherish one. Even now I cannot tell for whom I have most pity, or who was closest to my mind. But three are dead, and one is sore stricken; neither is there anything in the world which can bring me comfort. Only this is there to do—to give the slain men seemly burial, and, if it may be, to heal their comrade of his wounds."

So, because of her great love and nobleness, the lady caused these three distressful knights to be buried well and worshipfully in a rich abbey. In that place she offered their Mass penny, and gave rich offerings of silver and of lights besides. May God have mercy on them in that day. As for the wounded knight she commanded him to be carried to her own chamber. She sent for surgeons, and gave him into their hands. These searched his wounds so skilfully, and tended him with so great care, that presently his hurt commenced to heal. Very often was the lady in the chamber, and very tenderly she cherished the stricken man. Yet ever she felt pity for the three Knights of the Sorrows, and ever she went heavily by reason of their deaths.

Now on a summer's day, the lady and the knight sat together after meat. She called to mind the sorrow that was hers; so that, in a space, her head fell upon her breast, and she gave herself altogether to her grief. The knight looked earnestly upon his dame. Well he might see that she was far away, and clearly he perceived the cause.

"Lady," said he, "you are in sorrow. Open now your grief to me. If you tell me what is in your heart perchance I may find you comfort."

"Fair friend," replied she, "I think of what is gone, and remember your companions, who are dead. Never was lady of my peerage, however fair and good and gracious, ever loved by four such valiant gentlemen, nor ever lost them in one single day. Save you—who were so maimed and in such peril—all are gone. Therefore I call to mind those who loved me so dearly, and am the saddest lady beneath the sun. To remember these things, of you four I shall make a Lay, and will call it the Lay of the Four Sorrows."

When the knight heard these words he made answer very swiftly, "Lady, name it not the Lay of the Four Sorrows, but, rather, the Lay of the Dolorous Knight. Would you hear the reason why it should bear this name? My three comrades have finished their course; they have nothing more to hope of their life. They are gone, and with them the pang of their great sorrow, and the knowledge of their enduring love for you. I alone have come, all amazed and fearful, from the net wherein they were taken, but I find my life more bitter than my comrades found the grave. I see you on your goings and comings about the house. I may speak with you both matins and vespers. But no other joy do I get—neither clasp nor kiss, nothing but a few empty, courteous words. Since all these evils are come upon me because of you, I choose death rather than life. For this reason your Lay should bear my name, and be called the Lay of the Dolorous Knight. He who would name it the Lay of the Four Sorrows would name it wrongly, and not according to the truth."

"By my faith," replied the lady, "this is a fair saying. So shall the song be known as the Lay of the Dolorous Knight."

Thus was the Lay conceived, made perfect, and brought to a fair birth. For this reason it came by its name; though to this day some call it the Lay of the Four Sorrows. Either name befits it well, for the story tells of both these matters, but it is the use and wont in this land to call it the Lay of the Dolorous Knight. Here it ends; no more is there to say. I heard no more, and nothing more I know. Perforce I bring my story to a close.

THE LAY OF ELIDUC

Now will I rehearse before you a very ancient Breton Lay. As the tale was told to me, so, in turn, will I tell it over again, to the best of my art and knowledge. Hearken now to my story, its why and its reason.

In Brittany there lived a knight, so courteous and so brave, that in all the realm there was no worthier lord than he. This knight was named Eliduc. He had wedded in his youth a noble lady of proud race and name. They had long dwelt together in peace and content, for their hearts were fixed on one another in faith and loyalty. Now it chanced that Eliduc sought his fortune in a far land, where there was a great war. There he loved a Princess, the daughter of the King and Queen of those parts. Guillardun was the maiden's name, and in all the realm was none more fair. The wife of Eliduc had to name, Guildeluec, in her own country. By reason of these two ladies their story is known as the Lay of Guildeluec and Guillardun, but at first it was rightly called the Lay of Eliduc. The name is a little matter; but if you hearken to me you shall learn the story of these three lovers, in its pity and its truth.

Eliduc had as lord and suzerain, the King of Brittany over Sea. The knight was greatly loved and cherished of his prince, by reason of his long and loyal service. When the King's business took him from his realm, Eliduc was his master's Justice and Seneschal. He governed the country well and wisely, and held it from the foe with a strong hand. Nevertheless, in spite of all, much evil was appointed unto him. Eliduc was a mighty hunter, and by the King's grace, he would chase the stag within the woods. He was cunning and fair as Tristan, and so wise in venery, that the oldest forester might not gainsay him in aught concerning the shaw. But by reason of malice and envy, certain men accused him to the King that he had meddled with the royal pleasaunce. The King bade Eliduc to avoid his Court. He gave no reason for his commandment, and the knight might learn nothing of the cause. Often he prayed the King that he might know whereof he was accused. Often he begged his lord not to heed the specious and crafty words of his foes. He called to mind the wounds he had gained in his master's wars, but was answered never a word. When Eliduc found that he might get no speech with his lord, it became his honour to depart. He returned to his house, and calling his friends around him, opened out to them this business of the King's wrath, in recompense for his faithful service.

"I did not reckon on a King's gratitude; but as the proverb says, it is useless for a farmer to dispute with the horse in his plough. The wise and virtuous man keeps faith to his lord, and bears goodwill to his neighbour, not for what he may receive in return."

Then the knight told his friends that since he might no longer stay in his own country, he should cross the sea to the realm of Logres, and sojourn there awhile, for his solace. His fief he placed in the hands of his wife, and he required of his men, and of all who held him dear, that they would serve her loyally. Having given good counsel to the utmost of his power, the knight prepared him for the road. Right heavy were his friends and kin, that he must go forth from amongst them.

Eliduc took with him ten knights of his household, and set out on his journey. His dame came with him so far as she was able, wringing her hands, and making much sorrow, at the departure of her husband. At the end he pledged good faith to her, as she to him, and so she returned to her own home. Eliduc went his way, till he came to a haven on the sea. He took ship, and sailed to the realm of Totenois, for many kings dwell in that country, and ever there were strife and war. Now, near to Exeter, in this land, there dwelt a King, right rich and strong, but old and very full of years. He had no son of his body, but one maid only, young, and of an age to wed. Since he would not bestow this damsel on a certain prince of his neighbours, this lord made mortal war upon his fellow, spoiling and wasting all his land. The ancient King, for surety, had set his daughter within a castle, fair and very strong. He had charged the sergeants not to issue forth from the gates, and for the rest there was none so bold as to seek to storm the keep, or even to joust about the barriers. When Eliduc was told of this quarrel, he needed to go no farther, and sojourned for awhile in the land. He turned over in his mind which of these princes dealt unjustly with his neighbour. Since he deemed that the agèd king was the more vexed and sorely pressed in the matter, he resolved to aid him to the best of his might, and to take arms in his service. Eliduc, therefore, wrote letters to the King, telling him that he had quitted his own country, and sought refuge in the King's realm. For his part he was willing to fight as a mercenary in the King's quarrel, and if a safe conduct were given him, he and the knights of his company would ride, forthwith, to their master's aid. This letter, Eliduc sent by the hands of his squires to the King. When the ancient lord had read the letter, he rejoiced greatly, and made much of the messengers. He summoned his constable, and commanded him swiftly to write out the safe conduct, that would bring the baron to his side. For the rest he bade that the messengers meetly should be lodged and apparelled, and that such money should be given them as would be suffcient to their needs. Then he sealed the safe conduct with his royal seal, and sent it to Eliduc, straightway, by a sure hand.

When Eliduc came in answer to the summons, he was received with great honour by the King. His lodging was appointed in the house of a grave and courteous burgess of the city, who bestowed the fairest chamber on his guest. Eliduc fared softly, both at bed and board. He called to his table such good knights as were in misease, by reason of prison or of war. He charged his men that none should be so bold as to take pelf or penny from the citizens of the town, during the first forty days of their sojourn. But on the third day, it was bruited about the streets, that the enemy were near at hand. The country folk deemed that they approached to invest the city, and to take the gates by storm. When the noise and clamour of the fearful burgesses came to the ears of Eliduc, he and his company donned their harness, and got to horse, as quickly as they might. Forty horsemen mounted with him; as to the rest, many lay sick or hurt within the city, and others were captives in the hands of the foe. These forty stout sergeants waited for no sounding of trumpets; they hastened to seek their captain at his lodging, and rode at his back through the city gate.

"Sir," said they, "where you go, there we will follow, and what you bid us, that shall we do."

"Friends," made answer the knight, "I thank you for your fellowship. There is no man amongst us but who wishes to molest the foe, and do them all the mischief that he is able. If we await them in the town, we defend ourselves with the shield, and not with the sword. To my mind it is better to fall in the field than to hide behind walls; but if any of you have a wiser counsel to offer, now let him speak."

"Sir," replied a soldier of the company, "through the wood, in good faith, there runs a path, right strict and narrow. It is the wont of the enemy to approach our city by this track. After their deeds of arms before the walls, it is their custom to return by the way they came, helmet on saddle bow, and hauberk unbraced. If we might catch them, unready in the path, we could trouble them very grievously, even though it be at the peril of our lives."

"Friends," answered Eliduc, "you are all the King's men, and are bound to serve him faithfully, even to the death. Come, now, with me where I will go, and do that thing which you shall see me do. I give you my word as a loyal gentleman, that no harm shall hap to any. If we gain spoil and riches from the foe, each shall have his lot in the ransom. At the least we may do them much hurt and mischief in this quarrel."

Eliduc set his men in ambush, near by that path, within the wood. He told over to them, like a cunning captain, the crafty plan he had devised, and taught them how to play their parts, and to call upon his name. When the foe had entered on that perilous path, and were altogether taken in the snare, Eliduc cried his name, and summoned his companions to bear themselves like men. This they did stoutly, and assailed their enemy so fiercely that he was dismayed beyond measure, and his line being broken, fled to the forest. In this fight was the constable taken, together with fifty and five other lords, who owned themselves prisoners, and were given to the keeping of the squires. Great was the spoil in horse and harness, and marvellous was the wealth they gained in gold and ransom. So having done such great deeds in so short a space, they returned to the city, joyous and content.

The King looked forth from a tower. He feared grievously for his men, and made his complaint of Eliduc, who—he deemed—had betrayed him in his need. Upon the road he saw a great company, charged and laden with spoil. Since the number of those who returned was more than those who went forth, the king knew not again his own. He came down from the tower, in doubt and sore trouble, bidding that the gates should be made fast, and that men should mount upon the walls. For such coil as this, there was slender warrant. A squire who was sent out, came back with all speed, and showed him of this adventure. He told over the story of the ambush, and the tale of the prisoners. He rehearsed how the constable was taken, and that many a knight was wounded, and many a brave man slain. When the King might give credence thereto, he had more joy than ever king before. He got him from his tower, and going before Eliduc, he praised him to his face, and rendered him the captives as a gift. Eliduc gave the King's bounty to his men. He bestowed on them besides, all the harness and the spoil; keeping, for his part, but three knights, who had won much honour in the battle. From this day the King loved and cherished Eliduc very dearly. He held the knight, and his company, for a full year in his service, and at the end of the year, such faith had he in the knight's loyalty, that he appointed him Seneschal and Constable of his realm.

Eliduc was not only a brave and wary captain; he was also a courteous gentleman, right goodly to behold.

That fair maiden, the daughter of the King, heard tell of his deeds, and desired to see his face, because of the good men spake of him. She sent her privy chamberlain to the knight, praying him to come to her house, that she might solace herself with the story of his deeds, for greatly she wondered that he had no care for her friendship. Eliduc gave answer to the chamberlain that he would ride forthwith, since much he desired to meet so high a dame. He bade his squire to saddle his destrier, and rode to the palace, to have speech with the lady. Eliduc stood without the lady's chamber, and prayed the chamberlain to tell the dame that he had come, according to her wish. The chamberlain came forth with a smiling face, and straightway led him in the chamber. When the princess saw the knight, she cherished him very sweetly, and welcomed him in the most honourable fashion. The knight gazed upon the lady, who was passing fair to see. He thanked her courteously, that she was pleased to permit him to have speech with so high a princess. Guillardun took Eliduc by the hand, and seated him upon the bed, near her side. They spake together of many things, for each found much to say. The maiden looked closely upon the knight, his face and semblance; to her heart she said that never before had she beheld so comely a man. Her eyes might find no blemish in his person, and Love knocked upon her heart, requiring her to love, since her time had come. She sighed, and her face lost its fair colour; but she cared only to hide her trouble from the knight, lest he should think her the less maidenly therefore. When they had talked together for a great space, Eliduc took his leave, and went his way. The lady would have kept him longer gladly, but since she did not dare, she allowed him to depart. Eliduc returned to his lodging, very pensive and deep in thought. He called to mind that fair maiden, the daughter of his King, who so sweetly had bidden him to her side, and had kissed him farewell, with sighs that were sweeter still. He repented him right earnestly that he had lived so long a while in the land without seeking her face, but promised that often he would enter her palace now. Then he remembered the wife whom he had left in his own house. He recalled the parting between them, and the covenant he made, that good faith and stainless honour should be ever betwixt the twain. But the maiden, from whom he came, was willing to take him as her knight! If such was her will, might any pluck him from her hand?

All night long, that fair maiden, the daughter of the King, had neither rest nor sleep. She rose up, very early in the morning, and commanding her chamberlain, opened out to him all that was in her heart. She leaned her brow against the casement.

"By my faith," she said, "I am fallen into a deep ditch, and sorrow has come upon me. I love Eliduc, the good knight, whom my father made his Seneschal. I love him so dearly that I turn the whole night upon my bed, and cannot close my eyes, nor sleep. If he assured me of his heart, and loved me again, all my pleasure should be found in his happiness. Great might be his profit, for he would become King of this realm, and little enough is it for his deserts, so courteous is he and wise. If he have nothing better than friendship to give me, I choose death before life, so deep is my distress."

When the princess had spoken what it pleased her to say, the chamberlain, whom she had bidden, gave her loyal counsel.

"Lady," said he, "since you have set your love upon this knight, send him now—if so it please you—some goodly gift-girdle or scarf or ring. If he receive the gift with delight, rejoicing in your favour, you may be assured that he loves you. There is no Emperor, under Heaven, if he were tendered your tenderness, but would go the more lightly for your grace."

The damsel hearkened to the counsel of her chamberlain, and made reply, "If only I knew that he desired my love! Did ever maiden woo her knight before, by asking whether he loved or hated her? What if he make of me a mock and a jest in the ears of his friends! Ah, if the secrets of the heart were but written on the face! But get you ready, for go you must, at once."

"Lady," answered the chamberlain, "I am ready to do your bidding."

"You must greet the knight a hundred times in my name, and will place my girdle in his hand, and this my golden ring."

When the chamberlain had gone upon his errand, the maiden was so sick at heart, that for a little she would have bidden him return. Nevertheless, she let him go his way, and eased her shame with words.

"Alas, what has come upon me, that I should put my heart upon a stranger. I know nothing of his folk, whether they be mean or high; nor do I know whether he will part as swiftly as he came. I have done foolishly, and am worthy of blame, since I have bestowed my love very lightly. I spoke to him yesterday for the first time, and now I pray him for his love. Doubtless he will make me a song! Yet if he be the courteous gentleman I believe him, he will understand, and not deal hardly with me. At least the dice are cast, and if he may not love me, I shall know myself the most woeful of ladies, and never taste of joy all the days of my life."

Whilst the maiden lamented in this fashion, the chamberlain hastened to the lodging of Eliduc. He came before the knight, and having saluted him in his lady's name, he gave to his hand the ring and the girdle. The knight thanked him earnestly for the gifts. He placed the ring upon his finger, and the girdle he girt about his body. He said no more to the chamberlain, nor asked him any questions; save only that he proffered him a gift. This the messenger might not have, and returned the way he came. The chamberlain entered in the palace and found the princess within her chamber. He greeted her on the part of the knight, and thanked her for her bounty.

"Diva, diva," cried the lady hastily, "hide nothing from me; does he love me, or does he not?"

"Lady," answered the chamberlain, "as I deem, he loves you, and truly. Eliduc is no cozener with words. I hold him for a discreet and prudent gentleman, who knows well how to hide what is in his heart. I gave him greeting in your name, and granted him your gifts. He set the ring upon his finger, and as to your girdle, he girt it upon him, and belted it tightly about his middle. I said no more to him, nor he to me; but if he received not your gifts in tenderness, I am the more deceived. Lady, I have told you his words: I cannot tell you his thoughts. Only, mark carefully what I am about to say. If Eliduc had not a richer gift to offer, he would not have taken your presents at my hand."

"It pleases you to jest," said the lady. "I know well that Eliduc does not altogether hate me. Since my only fault is to cherish him too fondly, should he hate me, he would indeed be blameworthy. Never again by you, or by any other, will I require him of aught, or look to him for comfort. He shall see that a maiden's love is no slight thing, lightly given, and lightly taken again—but, perchance, he will not dwell in the realm so long as to know of the matter."

"Lady, the knight has covenanted to serve the King, in all loyalty, for the space of a year. You have full leisure to tell, whatever you desire him to learn."

When the maiden heard that Eliduc remained in the country, she rejoiced very greatly. She was glad that the knight would sojourn awhile in her city, for she knew naught of the torment he endured, since first he looked upon her. He had neither peace nor delight, for he could not get her from his mind. He reproached himself bitterly. He called to remembrance the covenant he made with his wife, when he departed from his own land, that he would never be false to his oath. But his heart was a captive now, in a very strong prison. He desired greatly to be loyal and honest, but he could not deny his love for the maiden—Guillardun, so frank and so fair.

Eliduc strove to act as his honour required. He had speech and sight of the lady, and did not refuse her kiss and embrace. He never spoke of love, and was diligent to offend in nothing. He was careful in this, because he would keep faith with his wife, and would attempt no matter against his King. Very grievously he pained himself, but at the end he might do no more. Eliduc caused his horse to be saddled, and calling his companions about him, rode to the castle to get audience of the King. He considered, too, that he might see his lady, and learn what was in her heart. It was the hour of meat, and the King having risen from table, had entered in his daughter's chamber. The King was at chess, with a lord who had but come from over sea. The lady sat near the board, to watch the movements of the game. When Eliduc came before the prince, he welcomed him gladly, bidding him to seat himself close at hand. Afterwards he turned to his daughter, and said, "Princess, it becomes you to have a closer friendship with this lord, and to treat him well and worshipfully. Amongst five hundred, there is no better knight than he."

When the maiden had listened demurely to her father's commandment, there was no gayer lady than she. She rose lightly to her feet, and taking the knight a little from the others, seated him at her side. They remained silent, because of the greatness of their love. She did not dare to speak the first, and to him the maid was more dreadful than a knight in mail. At the end Eliduc thanked her courteously for the gifts she had sent him; never was grace so precious and so kind. The maiden made answer to the knight, that very dear to her was the use he had found for her ring, and the girdle with which he had belted his body. She loved him so fondly that she wished him for her husband. If she might not have her wish, one thing she knew well, that she would take no living man, but would die unwed. She trusted he would not deny her hope.

"Lady," answered the knight, "I have great joy in your love, and thank you humbly for the goodwill you bear me. I ought indeed to be a happy man, since you deign to show me at what price you value our friendship. Have you remembered that I may not remain always in your realm? I covenanted with the King to serve him as his man for the space of one year. Perchance I may stay longer in his service, for I would not leave him till his quarrel be ended. Then I shall return to my own land; so, fair lady, you permit me to say farewell."

The maiden made answer to her knight, "Fair friend, right sweetly I thank you for your courteous speech. So apt a clerk will know, without more words, that he may have of me just what he would. It becomes my love to give faith to all you say."

The two lovers spoke together no further; each was well assured of what was in the other's heart. Eliduc rode back to his lodging, right joyous and content. Often he had speech with his friend, and passing great was the love which grew between the twain.

Eliduc pressed on the war so fiercely that in the end he took captive the King who troubled his lord, and had delivered the land from its foes. He was greatly praised of all as a crafty captain in the field, and a hardy comrade with the spear. The poor and the minstrel counted him a generous knight. About this time that King, who had bidden Eliduc avoid his realm, sought diligently to find him. He had sent three messengers beyond the seas to seek his ancient Seneschal. A strong enemy had wrought him much grief and loss. All his castles were taken from him, and all his country was a spoil to the foe. Often and sorely he repented him of the evil counsel to which he had given ear. He mourned the absence of his mightiest knight, and drove from his councils those false lords who, for malice and envy, had defamed him. These he outlawed forever from his realm. The King wrote letters to Eliduc, conjuring him by the loving friendship that was once between them, and summoning him as a vassal is required of his lord, to hasten to his aid, in that his bitter need. When Eliduc heard these tidings they pressed heavily upon him, by reason of the grievous love he bore the dame. She, too, loved him with a woman's whole heart. Between the two there was nothing but the purest love and tenderness. Never by word or deed had they spoiled their friendship.

To speak a little closely together; to give some fond and foolish gift; this was the sum of their love. In her wish and hope the maiden trusted to hold the knight in her land, and to have him as her lord. Naught she deemed that he was wedded to a wife beyond the sea.

"Alas," said Eliduc, "I have loitered too long in this country, and have gone astray. Here I have set my heart on a maiden, Guillardun, the daughter of the King, and she, on me. If, now, we part, there is no help that one, or both, of us, must die. Yet go I must. My lord requires me by letters, and by the oath of fealty that I have sworn. My own honour demands that I should return to my wife. I dare not stay; needs must I go. I cannot wed my lady, for not a priest in Christendom would make us man and wife. All things turn to blame. God, what a tearing asunder will our parting be! Yet there is one who will ever think me in the right, though I be held in scorn of all. I will be guided by her wishes, and what she counsels that will I do. The King, her sire, is troubled no longer by any war. First, I will go to him, praying that I may return to my own land, for a little, because of the need of my rightful lord. Then I will seek out the maiden, and show her the whole business. She will tell me her desire, and I shall act according to her wish."

The knight hesitated no longer as to the path he should follow. He went straight to the King, and craved leave to depart. He told him the story of his lord's distress, and read, and placed in the King's hands, the letters calling him back to his home. When the King had read the writing, and knew that Eliduc purposed to depart, he was passing sad and heavy. He offered the knight the third part of his kingdom, with all the treasure that he pleased to ask, if he would remain at his side. He offered these things to the knight—these, and the gratitude of all his days besides.

"Do not tempt me, sire," replied the knight. "My lord is in such deadly peril, and his letters have come so great a way to require me, that go I must to aid him in his need. When I have ended my task, I will return very gladly, if you care for my services, and with me a goodly company of knights to fight in your quarrels."

The King thanked Eliduc for his words, and granted him graciously the leave that he demanded. He gave him, moreover, all the goods of his house; gold and silver, hound and horses, silken cloths, both rich and fair, these he might have at his will. Eliduc took of them discreetly, according to his need. Then, very softly, he asked one other gift. If it pleased the King, right willingly would he say farewell to the princess, before he went. The King replied that it was his pleasure, too. He sent a page to open the door of the maiden's chamber, and to tell her the knight's request. When she saw him, she took him by the hand, and saluted him very sweetly. Eliduc was the more fain of counsel than of claspings. He seated himself by the maiden's side, and as shortly as he might, commenced to show her of the business. He had done no more than read her of his letters, than her face lost its fair colour, and near she came to swoon. When Eliduc saw her about to fall, he knew not what he did, for grief. He kissed her mouth, once and again, and wept above her, very tenderly. He took, and held her fast in his arms, till she had returned from her swoon.

"Fair dear friend," said he softly, "bear with me while I tell you that you are my life and my death, and in you is all my comfort. I have bidden farewell to your father, and purposed to go back to my own land, for reason of this bitter business of my lord. But my will is only in your pleasure, and whatever the future brings me, your counsel I will do."

"Since you cannot stay," said the maiden, "take me with you, wherever you go. If not, my life is so joyless without you, that I would wish to end it with my knife."

Very sweetly made answer Sir Eliduc, for in honesty he loved honest maid, "Fair friend, I have sworn faith to your father, and am his man. If I carried you with me, I should give the lie to my troth. Let this covenant be made between us. Should you give me leave to return to my own land I swear to you on my honour as a knight, that I will come again on any day that you shall name. My life is in your hands. Nothing on earth shall keep me from your side, so only that I have life and health."

Then she, who loved so fondly, granted her knight permission to depart, and fixed the term, and named the day for his return. Great was their sorrow that the hour had come to bid farewell. They gave rings of gold for remembrance, and sweetly kissed adieu. So they severed from each other's arms.

Eliduc sought the sea, and with a fair wind, crossed swiftly to the other side. His lord was greatly content to learn the tidings of his knight's return. His friends and his kinsfolk came to greet him, and the common folk welcomed him very gladly. But, amongst them all, none was so blithe at his homecoming as the fair and prudent lady who was his wife. Despite this show of friendship, Eliduc was ever sad, and deep in thought. He went heavily, till he might look upon his friend. He felt no happiness, nor made pretence of any, till he should meet with her again. His wife was sick at heart, because of the coldness of her husband. She took counsel with her soul, as to what she had done amiss. Often she asked him privily, if she had come short or offended in any measure, whilst he was without the realm. If she was accused by any, let him tell her the accusation, that she might purge herself of the offence.

"Wife," answered Eliduc, "neither I, nor any other, charge you with aught that is against your honour to do. The cause of my sorrow is in myself. I have pledged my faith to the King of that country, from whence I come, that I will return to help him in his need. When my lord the King has peace in his realm, within eight days I shall be once more upon the sea. Great travail I must endure, and many pains I shall suffer, in readiness for that hour. Return I must, and till then I have no mind for anything but toil; for I will not give the lie to my plighted word."

Eliduc put his fief once more in the hands of his dame. He sought his lord, and aided him to the best of his might. By the counsel and prowess of the knight, the King came again into his own. When the term appointed by his lady, and the day she named for his return drew near, Eliduc wrought in such fashion that peace was accorded between the foes. Then the knight made him ready for his journey, and took thought to the folk he should carry with him. His choice fell on two of his nephews, whom he loved very dearly, and on a certain chamberlain of his household. These were trusted servitors, who were of his inmost mind, and knew much of his counsel. Together with these went his squires, these only, for Eliduc had no care to take many. All these, nephew and squire and chamberlain, Eliduc made to promise, and confirm by an oath, that they would reveal nothing of his business.

The company put to sea without further tarrying, and, crossing quickly, came to that land where Eliduc so greatly desired to be. The knight sought a hostel some distance from the haven, for he would not be seen of any, nor have it bruited that Eliduc was returned. He called his chamberlain, and sent him to his friend, bearing letters that her knight had come, according to the covenant that had been made. At nightfall, before the gates were made fast, Eliduc issued forth from the city, and followed after his messenger. He had clothed himself in mean apparel, and rode at a footpace straight to the city, where dwelt the daughter of the King. The chamberlain arrived before the palace, and by dint of asking and prying, found himself within the lady's chamber. He saluted the maiden, and told her that her lover was near. When Guillardun heard these tidings she was astonied beyond measure, and for joy and pity wept right tenderly. She kissed the letters of her friend, and the messenger who brought such welcome tidings. The chamberlain prayed the lady to attire and make her ready to join her friend. The day was spent in preparing for the adventure, according to such plan as had been devised. When dark was come, and all was still, the damsel stole forth from the palace, and the chamberlain with her. For fear that any man should know her again, the maiden had hidden, beneath a riding cloak, her silken gown, embroidered with gold. About the space of a bow shot from the city gate, there was a coppice standing within a fair meadow. Near by this wood,

Eliduc and his comrades awaited the coming of Guillardun. When Eliduc saw the lady, wrapped in her mantle, and his chamberlain leading her by the hand, he got from his horse, and kissed her right tenderly. Great joy had his companions at so fair a sight. He set her on the horse, and climbing before her, took bridle in glove, and returned to the haven, with all the speed he might. He entered forthwith in the ship, which put to sea, having on board none, save Eliduc, his men, and his lady, Guillardun. With a fair wind, and a quiet hour, the sailors thought that they would swiftly come to shore. But when their journey was near its end, a sudden tempest arose on the sea. A mighty wind drove them far from their harbourage, so that their rudder was broken, and their sail torn from the mast. Devoutly they cried on St. Nicholas, St. Clement, and Madame St. Mary, to aid them in this peril. They implored the Mother that she would approach her Son, not to permit them to perish, but to bring them to the harbour where they would come. Without sail or oar, the ship drifted here and there, at the mercy of the storm. They were very close to death, when one of the company, with a loud voice began to cry, "What need is there of prayers! Sir, you have with you, her, who brings us to our death. We shall never win to land, because you, who already have a faithful wife, seek to wed this foreign woman, against God and His law, against honour and your plighted troth. Grant us to cast her in the sea, and straightway the winds and the waves will be still."

When Eliduc heard these words he was like to come to harm for rage.

"Bad servant and felon traitor," he cried, "you should pay dearly for your speech, if I might leave my lady."

Eliduc held his friend fast in his arms, and cherished her as well as he was able. When the lady heard that her knight was already wedded in his own realm, she swooned where she lay. Her face became pale and discoloured; she neither breathed nor sighed, nor could any bring her any comfort. Those who carried her to a sheltered place, were persuaded that she was but dead, because of the fury of the storm. Eliduc was passing heavy. He rose to his feet, and hastening to his squire, smote him so grievously with an oar, that he fell senseless on the deck. He haled him by his legs to the side of the ship and flung the body in the sea, where it was swiftly swallowed by the waves. He went to the broken rudder, and governed the nave so skilfully, that it presently drew to land. So, having come to their fair haven, they cast anchor, and made fast their bridge to the shore. Dame Guillardun lay yet in her swoon, and seemed no other than if she were really dead. Eliduc's sorrow was all the more, since he deemed that he had slain her with his hand. He inquired of his companions in what near place they might lay the lady to her rest, "for I will not bid her farewell, till she is put in holy ground with such pomp and rite as befit the obsequies of the daughter of a King." His comrades answered him never a word, for they were all bemused by reason of what had befallen. Eliduc, therefore, considered within himself to what place he should carry the lady. His own home was so near the haven where he had come, that very easily they could ride there before evening. He called to mind that in his realm there was a certain great forest, both long and deep. Within this wood there was a little chapel, served by a holy hermit for forty years, with whom Eliduc had oftimes spoken.

"To this holy man," he said, "I will bear my lady. In his chapel he shall bury her sweet body. I will endow him so richly of my lands, that upon her chantry shall be founded a mighty abbey. There some convent of monks or nuns or canons shall ever hold her in remembrance, praying God to grant her mercy in His day."

Eliduc got to horse, but first took oath of his comrades that never, by them, should be discovered, that which they should see. He set his friend before him on the palfrey, and thus the living and the dead rode together, till they had entered the wood, and come before the chapel. The squires called and beat upon the door, but it remained fast, and none was found to give them any answer. Eliduc bade that one should climb through a window, and open the door from within. When they had come within the chapel they found a new made tomb, and writ thereon, that the holy hermit having finished his course, was made perfect, eight days before Passing sad was Eliduc, and esmayed. His companions would have digged a second grave, and set therein, his friend; but the knight would in no wise consent, for—he said— he purposed to take counsel of the priests of his country, as to building some church or abbey above her tomb. "At this hour we will but lay her body before the altar, and commend her to God His holy keeping." He commanded them to bring their mantles and make a bed upon the altar-pace. Thereon they laid the maiden, and having wrapped her close in her lover's cloak, left her alone. When the moment came for Eliduc to take farewell of his lady, he deemed that his own last hour had come. He kissed her eyes and her face.

"Fair friend," said he, "if it be pleasing to God, never will I bear sword or lance again, or seek the pleasures of this mortal world. Fair friend, in an ill hour you saw me! Sweet lady, in a bitter hour you followed me to death! Fairest, now were you a queen, were it not for the pure and loyal love you set upon me? Passing sad of heart am I for you, my friend. The hour that I have seen you in your shroud, I will take the habit of some holy order, and every day, upon your tomb, I will tell over the chaplet of my sorrow."

Having taken farewell of the maiden, Eliduc came forth from the chapel, and closed the doors. He sent messages to his wife, that he was returning to his house, but weary and overborne. When the dame heard these tidings, she was happy in her heart, and made ready to greet him. She received her lord tenderly; but little joy came of her welcome, for she got neither smiles in answer, nor tender words in return. She dared not inquire the reason, during the two days Eliduc remained in the house. The knight heard Mass very early in the morning, and then set forth on the road leading to the chapel where the maiden lay. He found her as he had parted, for she had not come back from her swoon, and there was neither stir in her, nor breath. He marvelled greatly, for he saw her, vermeil and white, as he had known her in life. She had lost none of her sweet colour, save that she was a little blanched. He wept bitterly above her, and entreated for her soul. Having made his prayer, he went again to his house.

On a day when Eliduc went forth, his wife called to her a varlet of her household, commanding him to follow his lord afar off, and mark where he went, and on what business. She promised to give him harness and horses, if he did according to her will. The varlet hid himself in the wood, and followed so cunningly after his lord, that he was not perceived. He watched the knight enter the chapel, and heard the cry and lamentation that he made. When Eliduc came out, the varlet hastened to his mistress, and told her what he had seen, the tears and dolour, and all that befell his lord within the hermitage. The lady summoned all her courage.

"We will go together, as soon as we may, to this hermitage. My lord tells me that he rides presently to the Court to speak with the King. I knew that my husband loved this dead hermit very tenderly, but I little thought that his loss would make him mad with grief."

The next day the dame let her lord go forth in peace. When, about noon, Eliduc rode to the Court to greet his King, the lady rose quickly, and carrying the varlet with her, went swiftly to the hermitage. She entered the chapel, and saw the bed upon the altar-pace, and the maiden thereon, like a new sprung rose. Stooping down the lady removed the mantle. She marked the rigid body, the long arms, and the frail white hands, with their slender fingers, folded on the breast. Thus she learned the secret of the sorrow of her lord. She called the varlet within the chapel, and showed him this wonder.

"Seest thou," she said, "this woman, who for beauty shineth as a gem! This lady, in her life, was the lover of my lord. It was for her that all his days were spoiled by grief. By my faith I marvel little at his sorrow, since I,

who am a woman too, will—for pity's sake or love—
never know joy again, having seen so fair a lady in the
dust."

So the wife wept above the body of the maiden.
Whilst the lady sat weeping, a weasel came from under
the altar, and ran across Guillardun's body. The varlet
smote it with his staff, and killed it as it passed. He took
the vermin and flung it away. The companion of this
weasel presently came forth to seek him. She ran to the
place where he lay, and finding that he would not get
him on his feet, seemed as one distraught. She went
forth from the chapel, and hastened to the wood, from
whence she returned quickly, bearing a vermeil flower
beneath her teeth. This red flower she placed within the
mouth of that weasel the varlet had slain, and
immediately he stood upon his feet. When the lady saw
this, she cried to the varlet,

"Throw, man, throw, and gain the flower."

The servitor flung his staff, and the weasels fled away,
leaving that fair flower upon the floor. The lady rose. She
took the flower, and returned with it swiftly to the altar
pace. Within the mouth of the maiden, she set a flower
that was more vermeil still. For a short space the dame
and the damsel were alike breathless. Then the maiden
came to herself, with a sigh. She opened her eyes, and
commenced to speak.

"Diva," she said, "have I slept so long, indeed!"

When the lady heard her voice she gave thanks to
God. She inquired of the maiden as to her name and
degree. The damsel made answer to her, "Lady, I was
born in Logres, and am daughter to the King of that
realm. Greatly there I loved a knight, named Eliduc, the

seneschal of my sire. We fled together from my home, to my own most grievous fault. He never told me that he was wedded to a wife in his own country, and he hid the matter so cunningly, that I knew naught thereof. When I heard tell of his dame, I swooned for pure sorrow. Now I find that this false lover, has, like a felon, betrayed me in a strange land. What will chance to a maiden in so foul a plight? Great is that woman's folly who puts her trust in man."

"Fair damsel," replied the lady, "there is nothing in the whole world that can give such joy to this felon, as to hear that you are yet alive. He deems that you are dead, and every day he beweeps your swoon in the chapel. I am his wife, and my heart is sick, just for looking on his sorrow. To learn the reason of his grief, I caused him to be followed, and that is why I have found you here. It is a great happiness for me to know that you live. You shall return with me to my home, and I will place you in the tenderness of your friend. Then I shall release him of his marriage troth, since it is my dearest hope to take the veil."

When the wife had comforted the maiden with such words, they went together to her own house. She called to her servitor, and bade him seek his lord. The varlet went here and there, till he lighted on Eliduc. He came before him, and showed him of all these things. Eliduc mounted straightway on his horse, and waiting neither for squire or companion, that same night came to his hall. When he found alive, her, who once was dead, Eliduc thanked his wife for so dear a gift. He rejoiced beyond measure, and of all his days, no day was more happy than this. He kissed the maiden often, and very sweetly she gave him again his kiss, for great was the joy between the twain. The dame looked on their happiness, and knew that her lord meetly had bestowed his love. She prayed him, therefore, that he would grant her leave to depart, since she would serve God as a cloistered nun. Of his wealth she craved such a portion as would permit her to found a convent. He would then be able to wed the maiden on whom his heart was set, for it was neither honest nor seemly that a man should maintain a wife with either hand.

Eliduc could do no otherwise than consent. He gave the permission she asked, and did all according to her will. He endowed the lady of his lands, near by that chapel and hermitage, within the wood. There he built a church with offices and refectory, fair to see. Much wealth he bestowed on the convent, in money and estate. When all was brought to a good end, the lady took the veil upon her head. Thirty other ladies entered in the house with her, and long she ruled them as their Abbess, right wisely and well.

Eliduc wedded with his friend, in great pomp, and passing rich was the marriage feast. They dwelt in unity together for many days, forever between them was perfect love. They walked uprightly, and gave alms of their goods, till such a time as it became them to turn to God. After much thought, Eliduc built a great church close beside his castle. He endowed it with all his gold and silver, and with the rest of his land. He set priests there, and holy layfolk also, for the business of the house, and the fair services of religion.

When all was builded and ordered, Eliduc offered himself, with them, that he—weak man—might serve the

omnipotent God. He set with the Abbess Guildeluec—
who once was his dame—that wife whom he loved so
dearly well. The Abbess received her as a sister, and
welcomed her right honourably. She admonished her in
the offices of God, and taught her of the rules and
practice of their holy Order. They prayed to God for
their friend, that He would grant him mercy in His day.
In turn, he entreated God for them. Messages came from
convent and monastery as to how they fared, so that
each might encourage the other in His way. Each strove
painfully, for himself and his, to love God the more
dearly, and to abide in His holy faith. Each made a good
end, and the mercy of God was abundantly made clear
to all.

Of the adventure of these three lovers, the courteous
Bretons made this Lay for remembrance, since they
deemed it a matter that men should not forget.

The Lay of the Nightingale

Now will I tell you a story, whereof the Breton harper already has made a Lay. Laustic, I deem, men name it in that country, which, being interpreted, means rossignol in French, and nightingale in good plain English.

In the realm of Brittany stands a certain rich and mighty city, called Saint Malo. There were citizens of this township two knights, so well spoken and reputed of all, that the city drew therefrom great profit and fame. The houses of these lords were very near the one to the other. One of the two knights had to wife a passing fair lady, right gracious of manner and sweet of tongue. Wondrous pleasure found this dame to array herself richly, after the wont and fashion of her time. The other knight was yet a bachelor. He was well accounted of amongst his fellows as a hardy knight and as an honourable man. He gave hospitality gladly. Largely he gained, largely he spent, and willingly bestowed gifts of all that he had.

This bachelor set his love upon his neighbour's wife. By reason of his urgent prayers, his long suit and service, and by reason that all men spake naught of him but praise—perchance, also, for reason that he was never far from her eye—presently this lady came to set her heart on him again. Though these two friends loved right tenderly, yet were they so private and careful in their loves that none perceived what was in their hearts. No man pried on them, or disturbed their goings and comings. These were the more easy to devise since the bachelor and the lady were such near neighbours. Their two houses stood side by side, hall and cellar and combles. Only between the gardens was built a high and ancient wall, of worn gray stone. When the lady sat within her bower, by leaning from the casement she and her friend might speak together, he to her, and she to him. They could also throw messages in writing, and divers pretty gifts, the one to the other. Little enough had they to displease them, and greatly were they at their ease, save only that they might not take their pleasure together, so often as their hearts had wished. For the dame was guarded very straitly when her husband was abroad. Yet not so strictly but that they might have word and speech, the now by night and now by day. At least, however close the watch and ward, none might hinder that at times these fair lovers stood within their casements, and looked fondly on the other's face.

Now after these friends had loved for a great space it chanced that the season became warm and sweet. It was the time when meadow and copse are green; when orchards grow white with bloom, and birds break into song as thickly as the bush to flower. It is the season when he who loves would win to his desire. Truly I tell you that the knight would have done all in his power to attain his wish, and the lady, for her part, yearned for sight and speech of her friend. At night, when the moon shone clearly in the sky, and her lord lay sleeping at her side, often the dame slipped softly from her bed, and hastening to the casement, leaned forth to have sight of him who watched. The greater part of the dark they kept vigil together, for very pleasant it is to look upon your friend, when sweeter things are denied.

This chanced so often, and the lady rose so frequently from her bed, that her lord was altogether wrathful, and many a time inquired the reason of her unrest.

"Husband," replied the dame, "there is no dearer joy in this world, than to hear the nightingale sing. It is to hearken to the song that rises so sweetly on the night, that I lean forth from the casement. What tune of harp or viol is half so fair! Because of my delight in his song, and of my desire to hear, I may not shut my eyes till it be morn."

When the husband heard the lady's words he laughed within himself for wrath and malice. He purposed that very soon the nightingale should sing within a net. So he bade the servants of his house to devise fillets and snares, and to set their cunning traps about the orchard. Not a chestnut tree nor hazel within the garth but was limed and netted for the caging of this bird. It was not long therefore ere the nightingale was taken, and the servants made haste to give him to the pleasure of their lord. Wondrous merry was the knight when he held him living in his hand. He went straightway to the chamber of his dame, and entering, said,

"Wife, are you within? Come near, for I must speak with you. Here is the nightingale, all limed and taken, who made vigil of your sleeping hours. Take now your rest in peace, for he will never disturb you more."

When the lady understood these words she was marvellously sorrowful and heavy. She prayed her lord to grant her the nightingale for a gift. But for all answer he wrung his neck with both hands so fiercely that the head was torn from the body. Then, right foully, he flung the bird upon the knees of the dame, in such fashion that her breast was sprinkled with the blood. So he departed, incontinent, from the chamber in a rage.

The lady took the little body in her hands, and wept his evil fate. She railed on those who with nets and snares had betrayed the nightingale to his death; for anger and hate beyond measure had gained hold on her heart.

"Alas," cried she, "evil is come upon me. Never again may I rise from my bed in the night, and watch from the casement, so that I may see my friend. One thing I know full well, that he will deem my love is no more set upon him. Woe to her who has none to give her counsel. This I will do. I will bestow the nightingale upon him, and send him tidings of the chance that has befallen."

So this doleful lady took a fair piece of white samite, broidered with gold, and wrought thereon the whole story of this adventure. In this silken cloth she wrapped the body of the little bird, and calling to her a trusty servant of her house, charged him with the message, and bade him bear it to her friend. The varlet went his way to the knight, and having saluted him on the part of the lady, he told over to him the story, and bestowed the nightingale upon him. When all had been rehearsed and shown to him, and he had well considered the matter, the knight was very dolent; yet in no wise would he avenge himself wrongfully. So he caused a certain coffret to be fashioned, made not of iron or steel, but of fine gold and fair stones, most rich and precious, right strongly clasped and bound. In this little chest he set the body of the nightingale, and having sealed the shrine, carried it upon him whenever his business took him abroad.

This adventure could not long be hid. Very swiftly it was noised about the country, and the Breton folk made a Lay thereon, which they called the Lay of the Laustic, in their own tongue.

THE LAY OF SIR LAUNFAL

I will tell you the story of another Lay. It relates the adventures of a rich and mighty baron, and the Breton calls it, the Lay of Sir Launfal.

King Arthur—that fearless knight and courteous lord—removed to Wales, and lodged at Caerleon-on-Usk, since the Picts and Scots did much mischief in the land. For it was the wont of the wild people of the north to enter in the realm of Logres, and burn and damage at their will. At the time of Pentecost, the King cried a great feast. Thereat he gave many rich gifts to his counts and barons, and to the Knights of the Round Table. Never were such worship and bounty shown before at any feast, for Arthur bestowed honours and lands on all his servants—save only on one. This lord, who was forgotten and misliked of the King, was named Launfal. He was beloved by many of the Court, because of his beauty and prowess, for he was a worthy knight, open of heart and heavy of hand. These lords, to whom their comrade was dear, felt little joy to see so stout a knight misprized. Sir Launfal was son to a King of high descent, though his heritage was in a distant land. He was of the

King's household, but since Arthur gave him naught, and he was of too proud a mind to pray for his due, he had spent all that he had. Right heavy was Sir Launfal, when he considered these things, for he knew himself taken in the toils. Gentles, marvel not overmuch hereat. Ever must the pilgrim go heavily in a strange land, where there is none to counsel and direct him in the path.

Now, on a day, Sir Launfal got him on his horse, that he might take his pleasure for a little. He came forth from the city, alone, attended by neither servant nor squire. He went his way through a green mead, till he stood by a river of clear running water. Sir Launfal would have crossed this stream, without thought of pass or ford, but he might not do so, for reason that his horse was all fearful and trembling. Seeing that he was hindered in this fashion, Launfal unbitted his steed, and let him pasture in that fair meadow, where they had come. Then he folded his cloak to serve him as a pillow, and lay upon the ground. Launfal lay in great misease, because of his heavy thoughts, and the discomfort of his bed. He turned from side to side, and might not sleep. Now as the knight looked towards the river he saw two damsels coming towards him; fairer maidens Launfal had never seen. These two maidens were richly dressed in kirtles closely laced and shapen to their persons and wore mantles of a goodly purple hue. Sweet and dainty were the damsels, alike in raiment and in face. The elder of these ladies carried in her hands a basin of pure gold, cunningly wrought by some crafty smith—very fair and precious was the cup; and the younger bore a towel of soft white linen. These maidens turned neither to the right hand nor to the left, but went directly to the place where Launfal lay. When Launfal saw that their business was with him, he stood upon his feet, like a discreet and courteous gentleman. After they had greeted the knight, one of the maidens delivered the message with which she was charged.

"Sir Launfal, my demoiselle, as gracious as she is fair, prays that you will follow us, her messengers, as she has a certain word to speak with you. We will lead you swiftly to her pavilion, for our lady is very near at hand. If you but lift your eyes you may see where her tent is spread."

Right glad was the knight to do the bidding of the maidens. He gave no heed to his horse, but left him at his provand in the meadow. All his desire was to go with the damsels, to that pavilion of silk and divers colours, pitched in so fair a place. Certainly neither Semiramis in the days of her most wanton power, nor Octavian, the Emperor of all the West, had so gracious a covering from sun and rain. Above the tent was set an eagle of gold, so rich and precious, that none might count the cost. The cords and fringes thereof were of silken thread, and the lances which bore aloft the pavilion were of refined gold. No King on earth might have so sweet a shelter, not though he gave in fee the value of his realm. Within this pavilion Launfal came upon the Maiden. Whiter she was than any altar lily, and more sweetly flushed than the new born rose in time of summer heat. She lay upon a bed with napery and coverlet of richer worth than could be furnished by a castle's spoil. Very fresh and slender showed the lady in her vesture of spotless linen. About her person she had drawn a mantle of ermine, edged with purple dye from the vats of Alexandria. By reason of the heat her raiment was unfastened for a little, and her throat and the rondure of her bosom showed whiter and more untouched than hawthorn in May. The knight came before the bed, and stood gazing on so sweet a sight. The Maiden beckoned him to draw near, and when he had seated himself at the foot of her couch, spoke her mind.

"Launfal," she said, "fair friend, it is for you that I have come from my own far land. I bring you my love. If you are prudent and discreet, as you are goodly to the view, there is no emperor nor count, nor king, whose day shall be so filled with riches and with mirth as yours."

When Launfal heard these words he rejoiced greatly, for his heart was litten by another's torch.

"Fair lady," he answered, "since it pleases you to be so gracious, and to dower so graceless a knight with your love, there is naught that you may bid me do—right or wrong, evil or good—that I will not do to the utmost of my power. I will observe your commandment, and serve in your quarrels. For you I renounce my father and my father's house. This only I pray, that I may dwell with you in your lodging, and that you will never send me from your side."

When the Maiden heard the words of him whom so fondly she desired to love, she was altogether moved, and granted him forthwith her heart and her tenderness. To her bounty she added another gift besides. Never might Launfal be desirous of aught, but he would have according to his wish. He might waste and spend at will and pleasure, but in his purse ever there was to spare.

No more was Launfal sad. Right merry was the pilgrim, since one had set him on the way, with such a gift, that the more pennies he bestowed, the more silver and gold were in his pouch.

But the Maiden had yet a word to say.

"Friend," she said, "hearken to my counsel. I lay this charge upon you, and pray you urgently, that you tell not to any man the secret of our love. If you show this matter, you will lose your friend, forever and a day. Never again may you see my face. Never again will you have seisin of that body, which is now so tender in your eyes."

Launfal plighted faith, that right strictly he would observe this commandment. So the Maiden granted him her kiss and her embrace, and very sweetly in that fair lodging passed the day till evensong was come.

Right loath was Launfal to depart from the pavilion at the vesper hour, and gladly would he have stayed, had he been able, and his lady wished.

"Fair friend," said she, "rise up, for no longer may you tarry. The hour is come that we must part. But one thing I have to say before you go. When you would speak with me I shall hasten to come before your wish. Well I deem that you will only call your friend where she may be found without reproach or shame of men. You may see me at your pleasure; my voice shall speak softly in your ear at will; but I must never be known of your comrades, nor must they ever learn my speech."

Right joyous was Launfal to hear this thing. He sealed the covenant with a kiss, and stood upon his feet. Then there entered the two maidens who had led him to the pavilion, bringing with them rich raiment, fitting for a knight's apparel. When Launfal had clothed himself therewith, there seemed no goodlier varlet under heaven, for certainly he was fair and true. After these maidens had refreshed him with clear water, and dried his hands upon the napkin, Launfal went to meat. His friend sat at table with him, and small will had he to refuse her courtesy. Very serviceably the damsels bore the meats, and Launfal and the Maiden ate and drank with mirth and content. But one dish was more to the knight's relish than any other. Sweeter than the dainties within his mouth, was the lady's kiss upon his lips.

When supper was ended, Launfal rose from table, for his horse stood waiting without the pavilion. The destrier was newly saddled and bridled, and showed proudly in his rich gay trappings. So Launfal kissed, and bade farewell, and went his way. He rode back towards the city at a slow pace. Often he checked his steed, and looked behind him, for he was filled with amazement, and all bemused concerning this adventure. In his heart he doubted that it was but a dream. He was altogether astonished, and knew not what to do. He feared that pavilion and Maiden alike were from the realm of faery.

Launfal returned to his lodging, and was greeted by servitors, clad no longer in ragged raiment. He fared richly, lay softly, and spent largely, but never knew how his purse was filled. There was no lord who had need of a lodging in the town, but Launfal brought him to his hall, for refreshment and delight. Launfal bestowed rich gifts. Launfal redeemed the poor captive. Launfal clothed in scarlet the minstrel. Launfal gave honour where honour was due. Stranger and friend alike he comforted at need. So, whether by night or by day, Launfal lived greatly at his ease. His lady, she came at will and pleasure, and, for the rest, all was added unto him.

Now it chanced, the same year, about the feast of St. John, a company of knights came, for their solace, to an orchard, beneath that tower where dwelt the Queen. Together with these lords went Gawain and his cousin, Yvain the fair. Then said Gawain, that goodly knight, beloved and dear to all,

"Lords, we do wrong to disport ourselves in this pleasaunce without our comrade Launfal. It is not well to slight a prince as brave as he is courteous, and of a lineage prouder than our own."

Then certain of the lords returned to the city, and finding Launfal within his hostel, entreated him to take his pastime with them in that fair meadow. The Queen looked out from a window in her tower, she and three ladies of her fellowship. They saw the lords at their pleasure, and Launfal also, whom well they knew. So the Queen chose of her Court thirty damsels—the sweetest of face and most dainty of fashion—and commanded that they should descend with her to take their delight in the garden. When the knights beheld this gay company of ladies come down the steps of the perron, they rejoiced beyond measure. They hastened before to lead them by the hand, and said such words in their ear as were seemly and pleasant to be spoken. Amongst these merry and courteous lords hasted not Sir Launfal. He drew apart from the throng, for with him time went heavily, till he might have clasp and greeting of his friend. The ladies of the Queen's fellowship seemed but kitchen wenches to his sight, in comparison with the loveliness of the maiden. When the Queen marked

Launfal go aside, she went his way, and seating herself upon the herb, called the knight before her. Then she opened out her heart.

"Launfal, I have honoured you for long as a worthy knight, and have praised and cherished you very dearly. You may receive a queen's whole love, if such be your care. Be content: he to whom my heart is given, has small reason to complain him of the alms."

"Lady," answered the knight, "grant me leave to go, for this grace is not for me. I am the King's man, and dare not break my troth. Not for the highest lady in the world, not even for her love, will I set this reproach upon my lord."

When the Queen heard this, she was full of wrath, and spoke many hot and bitter words.

"Launfal," she cried, "well I know that you think little of woman and her love. There are sins more black that a man may have upon his soul. Traitor you are, and false. Right evil counsel gave they to my lord, who prayed him to suffer you about his person. You remain only for his harm and loss."

Launfal was very dolent to hear this thing. He was not slow to take up the Queen's glove, and in his haste spake words that he repented long, and with tears.

"Lady," said he, "I am not of that guild of which you speak. Neither am I a despiser of woman, since I love, and am loved, of one who would bear the prize from all the ladies in the land. Dame, know now and be persuaded, that she, whom I serve, is so rich in state, that the very meanest of her maidens, excels you, Lady Queen, as much in clerkly skill and goodness, as in sweetness of body and face, and in every virtue."

The Queen rose straightway to her feet, and fled to her chamber, weeping. Right wrathful and heavy was she, because of the words that had besmirched her. She lay sick upon her bed, from which, she said, she would never rise, till the King had done her justice, and righted this bitter wrong. Now the King that day had taken his pleasure within the woods. He returned from the chase towards evening, and sought the chamber of the Queen. When the lady saw him, she sprang from her bed, and kneeling at his feet, pleaded for grace and pity. Launfal—she said—had shamed her, since he required her love. When she had put him by, very foully had he reviled her, boasting that his love was already set on a lady, so proud and noble, that her meanest wench went more richly, and smiled more sweetly, than the Queen. Thereat the King waxed marvellously wrathful, and swore a great oath that he would set Launfal within a fire, or hang him from a tree, if he could not deny this thing, before his peers.

Arthur came forth from the Queen's chamber, and called to him three of his lords. These he sent to seek the knight who so evilly had entreated the Queen. Launfal, for his part, had returned to his lodging, in a sad and sorrowful case. He saw very clearly that he had lost his friend, since he had declared their love to men. Launfal sat within his chamber, sick and heavy of thought. Often he called upon his friend, but the lady would not hear his voice. He bewailed his evil lot, with tears; for grief he came nigh to swoon; a hundred times he implored the Maiden that she would deign to speak with her knight. Then, since the lady yet refrained from speech, Launfal cursed his hot and unruly tongue. Very near he came to ending all this trouble with his knife. Naught he found to do but to wring his hands, and call upon the Maiden, begging her to forgive his trespass, and to talk with him again, as friend to friend.

But little peace is there for him who is harassed by a King. There came presently to Launfal's hostel those three barons from the Court. These bade the knight forthwith to go with them to Arthur's presence, to acquit him of this wrong against the Queen. Launfal went forth, to his own deep sorrow. Had any man slain him on the road, he would have counted him his friend. He stood before the King, downcast and speechless, being dumb by reason of that great grief, of which he showed the picture and image.

Arthur looked upon his captive very evilly.

"Vassal," said he, harshly, "you have done me a bitter wrong. It was a foul deed to seek to shame me in this ugly fashion, and to smirch the honour of the Queen. Is it folly or lightness which leads you to boast of that lady, the least of whose maidens is fairer, and goes more richly, than the Queen?"

Launfal protested that never had he set such shame upon his lord. Word by word he told the tale of how he denied the Queen, within the orchard. But concerning that which he had spoken of the lady, he owned the truth, and his folly. The love of which he bragged was now lost to him, by his own exceeding fault. He cared little for his life, and was content to obey the judgment of the Court.

Right wrathful was the King at Launfal's words. He conjured his barons to give him such wise counsel herein, that wrong might be done to none. The lords did the King's bidding, whether good came of the matter, or evil. They gathered themselves together, and appointed a certain day that Launfal should abide the judgment of his peers. For his part Launfal must give pledge and surety to his lord, that he would come before this judgment in his own body. If he might not give such surety then he should be held captive till the appointed day. When the lords of the King's household returned to tell him of their counsel, Arthur demanded that Launfal should put such pledge in his hand, as they had said. Launfal was altogether mazed and bewildered at this judgment, for he had neither friend nor kindred in the land. He would have been set in prison, but Gawain came first to offer himself as his surety, and with him, all the knights of his fellowship. These gave into the King's hand as pledge, the fiefs and lands that they held of his Crown. The King having taken pledges from the sureties, Launfal returned to his lodging, and with him certain knights of his company. They blamed him greatly because of his foolish love, and chastened him grievously by reason of the sorrow he made before men. Every day they came to his chamber, to know of his meat and drink, for much they feared that presently he would become mad.

The lords of the household came together on the day appointed for this judgment. The King was on his chair, with the Queen sitting at his side. The sureties brought Launfal within the hall, and rendered him into the hands of his peers. Right sorrowful were they because of his plight. A great company of his fellowship did all that they were able to acquit him of this charge. When all was set out, the King demanded the judgment of the

Court, according to the accusation and the answer. The barons went forth in much trouble and thought to consider this matter. Many amongst them grieved for the peril of a good knight in a strange land; others held that it were well for Launfal to suffer, because of the wish and malice of their lord. Whilst they were thus perplexed, the Duke of Cornwall rose in the council, and said,

"Lords, the King pursues Launfal as a traitor, and would slay him with the sword, by reason that he bragged of the beauty of his maiden, and roused the jealousy of the Queen. By the faith that I owe this company, none complains of Launfal, save only the King. For our part we would know the truth of this business, and do justice between the King and his man. We would also show proper reverence to our own liege lord. Now, if it be according to Arthur's will, let us take oath of Launfal, that he seek this lady, who has put such strife between him and the Queen. If her beauty be such as he has told us, the Queen will have no cause for wrath. She must pardon Launfal for his rudeness, since it will be plain that he did not speak out of a malicious heart. Should Launfal fail his word, and not return with the lady, or should her fairness fall beneath his boast, then let him be cast off from our fellowship, and be sent forth from the service of the King."

This counsel seemed good to the lords of the household. They sent certain of his friends to Launfal, to acquaint him with their judgment, bidding him to pray his damsel to the Court, that he might be acquitted of this blame. The knight made answer that in no wise could he do this thing. So the sureties returned before the judges, saying that Launfal hoped neither for refuge nor for succour from the lady, and Arthur urged them to a speedy ending, because of the prompting of the Queen.

The judges were about to give sentence upon Launfal, when they saw two maidens come riding towards the palace, upon two white ambling palfreys. Very sweet and dainty were these maidens, and richly clothed in garments of crimson sendal, closely girt and fashioned to their bodies. All men, old and young, looked willingly upon them, for fair they were to see. Gawain, and three knights of his company, went straight to Launfal, and showed him these maidens, praying him to say which of them was his friend. But he answered never a word. The maidens dismounted from their palfreys, and coming before the dais where the King was seated, spake him fairly, as they were fair.

"Sire, prepare now a chamber, hung with silken cloths, where it is seemly for my lady to dwell; for she would lodge with you awhile."

This gift the King granted gladly. He called to him two knights of his household, and bade them bestow the maidens in such chambers as were fitting to their degree. The maidens being gone, the King required of his barons to proceed with their judgment, saying that he had sore displeasure at the slowness of the cause.

"Sire," replied the barons, "we rose from Council, because of the damsels who entered in the hall. We will at once resume the sitting, and give our judgment without more delay."

The barons again were gathered together, in much thought and trouble, to consider this matter. There was great strife and dissension amongst them, for they knew not what to do. In the midst of all this noise and tumult, there came two other damsels riding to the hall on two Spanish mules. Very richly arrayed were these damsels in raiment of fine needlework, and their kirtles were covered by fresh fair mantles, embroidered with gold. Great joy had Launfal's comrades when they marked these ladies. They said between themselves that doubtless they came for the succour of the good knight. Gawain, and certain of his company, made haste to Launfal, and said, "Sir, be not cast down. Two ladies are near at hand, right dainty of dress, and gracious of person. Tell us truly, for the love of God, is one of these your friend?"

But Launfal answered very simply that never before had he seen these damsels with his eyes, nor known and loved them in his heart.

The maidens dismounted from their mules, and stood before Arthur, in the sight of all. Greatly were they praised of many, because of their beauty, and of the colour of their face and hair. Some there were who deemed already that the Queen was overborne.

The elder of the damsels carried herself modestly and well, and sweetly told over the message wherewith she was charged.

"Sire, make ready for us chambers, where we may abide with our lady, for even now she comes to speak with thee."

The King commanded that the ladies should be led to their companions, and bestowed in the same honourable fashion as they. Then he bade the lords of his household to consider their judgment, since he would endure no further respite. The Court already had given too much time to the business, and the Queen was growing wrathful, because of the blame that was hers. Now the judges were about to proclaim their sentence, when, amidst the tumult of the town, there came riding to the palace the flower of all the ladies of the world. She came mounted upon a palfrey, white as snow, which carried her softly, as though she loved her burden. Beneath the sky was no goodlier steed, nor one more gentle to the hand. The harness of the palfrey was so rich, that no king on earth might hope to buy trappings so precious, unless he sold or set his realm in pledge. The Maiden herself showed such as I will tell you. Passing slim was the lady, sweet of bodice and slender of girdle. Her throat was whiter than snow on branch, and her eyes were like flowers in the pallor of her face. She had a witching mouth, a dainty nose, and an open brow. Her eyebrows were brown, and her golden hair parted in two soft waves upon her head. She was clad in a shift of spotless linen, and above her snowy kirtle was set a mantle of royal purple, clasped upon her breast. She carried a hooded falcon upon her glove, and a greyhound followed closely after. As the Maiden rode at a slow pace through the streets of the city, there was none, neither great nor small, youth nor sergeant, but ran forth from his house, that he might content his heart with so great beauty. Every man that saw her with his eyes, marvelled at a fairness beyond that of any earthly woman. Little he cared for any mortal maiden, after he had seen this sight. The friends of Sir Launfal hastened to the knight, to tell him of his lady's succour, if so it were according to God's will.

"Sir comrade, truly is not this your friend? This lady is neither black nor golden, mean nor tall. She is only the most lovely thing in all the world."

When Launfal heard this, he sighed, for by their words he knew again his friend. He raised his head, and as the blood rushed to his face, speech flowed from his lips.

"By my faith," cried he, "yes, she is indeed my friend. It is a small matter now whether men slay me, or set me free; for I am made whole of my hurt just by looking on her face."

The Maiden entered in the palace—where none so fair had come before—and stood before the King, in the presence of his household. She loosed the clasp of her mantle, so that men might the more easily perceive the grace of her person. The courteous King advanced to meet her, and all the Court got them on their feet, and pained themselves in her service. When the lords had gazed upon her for a space, and praised the sum of her beauty, the lady spake to Arthur in this fashion, for she was anxious to begone.

"Sire, I have loved one of thy vassals—the knight who stands in bonds, Sir Launfal. He was always misprized in thy Court, and his every action turned to blame. What he said, that thou knowest; for over hasty was his tongue before the Queen. But he never craved her in love, however loud his boasting. I cannot choose that he should come to hurt or harm by me. In the hope of freeing Launfal from his bonds, I have obeyed thy summons. Let now thy barons look boldly upon my face, and deal justly in this quarrel between the Queen and me."

The King commanded that this should be done, and looking upon her eyes, not one of the judges but was persuaded that her favour exceeded that of the Queen.

Since then Launfal had not spoken in malice against his lady, the lords of the household gave him again his sword. When the trial had come thus to an end the Maiden took her leave of the King, and made her ready to depart. Gladly would Arthur have had her lodge with him for a little, and many a lord would have rejoiced in her service, but she might not tarry. Now without the hall stood a great stone of dull marble, where it was the wont of lords, departing from the Court, to climb into the saddle, and Launfal by the stone. The Maiden came forth from the doors of the palace, and mounting on the stone, seated herself on the palfrey, behind her friend. Then they rode across the plain together, and were no more seen.

The Bretons tell that the knight was ravished by his lady to an island, very dim and very fair, known as Avalon. But none has had speech with Launfal and his faery love since then, and for my part I can tell you no more of the matter.

The Lay of the Two Lovers

Once upon a time there lived in Normandy two lovers, who were passing fond, and were brought by Love to Death. The story of their love was bruited so abroad, that the Bretons made a song in their own tongue, and named this song the Lay of the Two Lovers.

In Neustria—that men call Normandy—there is verily a high and marvellously great mountain, where lie the relics of the Two Children. Near this high place the King of those parts caused to be built a certain fair and cunning city, and since he was lord of the Pistrians, it was known as Pistres. The town yet endures, with its towers and houses, to bear witness to the truth; moreover the country thereabouts is known to us all as the Valley of Pistres.

This King had one fair daughter, a damsel sweet of face and gracious of manner, very near to her father's heart, since he had lost his Queen. The maiden increased in years and favour, but he took no heed to her trothing, so that men—yea, even his own people—blamed him greatly for this thing. When the King heard thereof he was passing heavy and dolent, and considered within himself how he might be delivered from this grief. So then, that none should carry off his child, he caused it to be proclaimed, both far and near, by script and trumpet, that he alone should wed the maid, who would bear her in his arms, to the pinnacle of the great and perilous mountain, and that without rest or stay. When this news was noised about the country, many came upon the quest. But strive as they would they might not enforce themselves more than they were able. However mighty they were of body, at the last they failed upon the mountain, and fell with their burden to the ground. Thus, for a while, was none so bold as to seek the high Princess.

Now in this country lived a squire, son to a certain count of that realm, seemly of semblance and courteous, and right desirous to win that prize, which was so coveted of all. He was a welcome guest at the Court, and the King talked with him very willingly. This squire had set his heart upon the daughter of the King, and many a time spoke in her ear, praying her to give him again the love he had bestowed upon her. So seeing him brave and courteous, she esteemed him for the gifts which gained him the favour of the King, and they loved together in their youth. But they hid this matter from all about the Court. This thing was very grievous to them, but the damoiseau thought within himself that it were good to bear the pains he knew, rather than to seek out others that might prove sharper still. Yet in the end, altogether distraught by love, this prudent varlet sought his friend, and showed her his case, saying that he urgently required of her that she would flee with him, for no longer could he endure the weariness of his days. Should he ask her of the King, well he knew that by reason of his love he would refuse the gift, save he bore her in his arms up the steep mount. Then the maiden made answer to her lover, and said,

"Fair friend, well I know you may not carry me to that high place. Moreover should we take to flight, my father would suffer wrath and sorrow beyond measure, and go heavily all his days. Certainly my love is too fond to plague him thus, and we must seek another counsel, for this is not to my heart. Hearken well. I have kindred in Salerno, of rich estate. For more than thirty years my aunt has studied there the art of medicine, and knows the secret gift of every root and herb. If you hasten to her, bearing letters from me, and show her your adventure, certainly she will find counsel and cure. Doubt not that she will discover some cunning simple, that will strengthen your body, as well as comfort your heart. Then return to this realm with your potion, and ask me at my father's hand. He will deem you but a stripling, and set forth the terms of his bargain, that to him alone shall I be given who knows how to climb the perilous mountain, without pause or rest, bearing his lady between his arms."

When the varlet heard this cunning counsel of the maiden, he rejoiced greatly, and thanking her sweetly for her rede, craved permission to depart. He returned to his own home, and gathering together a goodly store of silken cloths most precious, he bestowed his gear upon the pack horses, and made him ready for the road. So with a little company of men, mounted on swift palfreys, and most privy to his mind, he arrived at Salerno. Now the squire made no long stay at his lodging, but as soon as he might, went to the damsel's kindred to open out his mind. He delivered to the aunt the letters he carried from his friend, and bewailed their evil case. When the dame had read these letters with him, line by line, she charged him to lodge with her awhile, till she might do according to his wish. So by her sorceries, and for the love of her maid, she brewed such a potion that no man, however wearied and outworn, but by drinking this philtre, would not be refreshed in heart and blood and bones. Such virtue had this medicine, directly it were drunken. This simple she poured within a little flacket, and gave it to the varlet, who received the gift with great joy and delight, and returned swiftly to his own land.

The varlet made no long sojourn in his home. He repaired straightway to the Court, and, seeking out the King, required of him his fair daughter in marriage, promising, for his part, that were she given him, he would bear her in his arms to the summit of the mount. The King was no wise wrath at his presumption. He smiled rather at his folly, for how should one so young and slender succeed in a business wherein so many mighty men had failed. Therefore he appointed a certain day for this judgment. Moreover he caused letters to be written to his vassals and his friends—passing none by— bidding them to see the end of this adventure. Yea, with public cry and sound of trumpet he bade all who would, come to behold the stripling carry his fair daughter to the pinnacle of the mountain. And from every region round about men came to learn the issue of this thing. But for her part the fair maiden did all that she was able to bring her love to a good end. Ever was it fast day and fleshless day with her, so that by any means she might lighten the burden that her friend must carry in his arms.

Now on the appointed day this young dansellon came very early to the appointed place, bringing the flacket with him. When the great company were fully met together, the King led forth his daughter before them; and all might see that she was arrayed in nothing but her smock. The varlet took the maiden in his arms, but first he gave her the flask with the precious brewage to carry, since for pride he might not endure to drink therefrom, save at utmost peril. The squire set forth at a great pace, and climbed briskly till he was halfway up the mount. Because of the joy he had in clasping his burden, he gave no thought to the potion. But she—she knew the strength was failing in his heart.

"Fair friend," said she, "well I know that you tire: drink now, I pray you, of the flacket, and so shall your manhood come again at need."

But the varlet answered,

"Fair love, my heart is full of courage; nor for any reason will I pause, so long as I can hold upon my way. It is the noise of all this folk—the tumult and the shouting—that makes my steps uncertain. Their cries distress me, I do not dare to stand."

But when two thirds of the course was won, the grasshopper would have tripped him off his feet. Urgently and often the maiden prayed him, saying,

"Fair friend, drink now of thy cordial."

But he would neither hear, nor give credence to her words. A mighty anguish filled his bosom. He climbed upon the summit of the mountain, and pained himself grievously to bring his journey to an end. This he might not do. He reeled and fell, nor could he rise again, for the heart had burst within his breast.

When the maiden saw her lover's piteous plight, she deemed that he had swooned by reason of his pain. She kneeled hastily at his side, and put the enchanted brewage to his lips, but he could neither drink nor speak, for he was dead, as I have told you. She bewailed his evil lot, with many shrill cries, and flung the useless flacket far away. The precious potion bestrewed the ground, making a garden of that desolate place. For many saving herbs have been found there since that day by the simple folk of that country, which from the magic philtre derived all their virtue.

But when the maiden knew that her lover was dead, she made such wondrous sorrow, as no man had ever seen. She kissed his eyes and mouth, and falling upon his body, took him in her arms, and pressed him closely to her breast. There was no heart so hard as not to be touched by her sorrow; for in this fashion died a dame, who was fair and sweet and gracious, beyond the wont of the daughters of men.

Now the King and his company, since these two lovers came not again, presently climbed the mountain to learn their end. But when the King came upon them lifeless, and fast in that embrace, incontinent he fell to the ground, bereft of sense. After his speech had returned to him, he was passing heavy, and lamented their doleful case, and thus did all his people with him.

Three days they kept the bodies of these two fair children from earth, with uncovered face. On the third day they sealed them fast in a goodly coffin of marble, and by the counsel of all men, laid them softly to rest on that mountain where they died. Then they departed from them, and left them together, alone.

Since this adventure of the Two Children this hill is known as the Mountain of the Two Lovers, and their story being bruited abroad, the Breton folk have made a Lay thereof, even as I have rehearsed before you.

THE LAY OF THE WEREWOLF

Amongst the tales I tell you once again, I would not forget the Lay of the Werewolf. Such beasts as he are known in every land. Bisclavaret he is named in Brittany; whilst the Norman calls him Garwal.

It is a certain thing, and within the knowledge of all, that many a christened man has suffered this change, and ran wild in woods, as a Werewolf. The Werewolf is a fearsome beast. He lurks within the thick forest, mad and horrible to see. All the evil that he may, he does. He goeth to and fro, about the solitary place, seeking man, in order to devour him. Hearken, now, to the adventure of the Werewolf, that I have to tell.

In Brittany there dwelt a baron who was marvellously esteemed of all his fellows. He was a stout knight, and a comely, and a man of office and repute. Right private was he to the mind of his lord, and dear to the counsel of his neighbours. This baron was wedded to a very worthy dame, right fair to see, and sweet of semblance. All his love was set on her, and all her love was given again to him. One only grief had this lady. For three whole days in every week her lord was absent from her side. She knew not where he went, nor on what errand. Neither did any of his house know the business which called him forth.

On a day when this lord was come again to his house, altogether joyous and content, the lady took him to task, right sweetly, in this fashion, "Husband," said she, "and fair, sweet friend, I have a certain thing to pray of you. Right willingly would I receive this gift, but I fear to anger you in the asking. It is better for me to have an empty hand, than to gain hard words."

When the lord heard this matter, he took the lady in his arms, very tenderly, and kissed her.

"Wife," he answered, "ask what you will. What would you have, for it is yours already?"

"By my faith," said the lady, "soon shall I be whole. Husband, right long and wearisome are the days that you spend away from your home. I rise from my bed in the morning, sick at heart, I know not why. So fearful am I, lest you do aught to your loss, that I may not find any comfort. Very quickly shall I die for reason of my dread. Tell me now, where you go, and on what business! How may the knowledge of one who loves so closely, bring you to harm?"

"Wife," made answer the lord, "nothing but evil can come if I tell you this secret. For the mercy of God do not require it of me. If you but knew, you would withdraw yourself from my love, and I should be lost indeed."

When the lady heard this, she was persuaded that her baron sought to put her by with jesting words. Therefore she prayed and required him the more urgently, with tender looks and speech, till he was overborne, and told her all the story, hiding naught.

"Wife, I become Bisclavaret. I enter in the forest, and live on prey and roots, within the thickest of the wood."

After she had learned his secret, she prayed and entreated the more as to whether he ran in his raiment, or went spoiled of vesture.

"Wife," said he, "I go naked as a beast."

"Tell me, for hope of grace, what you do with your clothing?"

"Fair wife, that will I never. If I should lose my raiment, or even be marked as I quit my vesture, then a Werewolf I must go for all the days of my life. Never again should I become man, save in that hour my clothing were given back to me. For this reason never will I show my lair."

"Husband," replied the lady to him, "I love you better than all the world. The less cause have you for doubting my faith, or hiding any tittle from me. What savour is here of friendship? How have I made forfeit of your love; for what sin do you mistrust my honour? Open now your heart, and tell what is good to be known."

So at the end, outwearied and overborne by her importunity, he could no longer refrain, but told her all.

"Wife," said he, "within this wood, a little from the path, there is a hidden way, and at the end thereof an ancient chapel, where oftentimes I have bewailed my lot. Near by is a great hollow stone, concealed by a bush, and there is the secret place where I hide my raiment, till I would return to my own home."

On hearing this marvel the lady became sanguine of visage, because of her exceeding fear. She dared no longer to lie at his side, and turned over in her mind, this way and that, how best she could get her from him. Now there was a certain knight of those parts, who, for a great while, had sought and required this lady for her love. This knight had spent long years in her service, but little enough had he got thereby, not even fair words, or a promise. To him the dame wrote a letter, and meeting, made her purpose plain.

"Fair friend," said she, "be happy. That which you have coveted so long a time, I will grant without delay. Never again will I deny your suit. My heart, and all I have to give, are yours, so take me now as love and dame."

Right sweetly the knight thanked her for her grace, and pledged her faith and fealty. When she had confirmed him by an oath, then she told him all this business of her lord—why he went, and what he became, and of his ravening within the wood. So she showed him of the chapel, and of the hollow stone, and of how to spoil the Werewolf of his vesture. Thus, by the kiss of his wife, was Bisclavaret betrayed. Often enough had he ravished his prey in desolate places, but from this journey he never returned. His kinsfolk and acquaintance came together to ask of his tidings, when this absence was noised abroad. Many a man, on many a day, searched the woodland, but none might find him, nor learn where Bisclavaret was gone.

The lady was wedded to the knight who had cherished her for so long a space. More than a year had passed since Bisclavaret disappeared. Then it chanced that the King would hunt in that selfsame wood where the Werewolf lurked. When the hounds were unleashed they ran this way and that, and swiftly came upon his scent. At the view the huntsman winded on his horn, and the whole pack were at his heels. They followed him from morn to eve, till he was torn and bleeding, and was all adread lest they should pull him down. Now the King was very close to the quarry, and when Bisclavaret looked upon his master, he ran to him for pity and for grace. He took the stirrup within his paws, and fawned upon the prince's foot. The King was very fearful at this sight, but presently he called his courtiers to his aid.

"Lords," cried he, "hasten hither, and see this marvellous thing. Here is a beast who has the sense of man. He abases himself before his foe, and cries for mercy, although he cannot speak. Beat off the hounds, and let no man do him harm. We will hunt no more today, but return to our own place, with the wonderful quarry we have taken."

The King turned him about, and rode to his hall, Bisclavaret following at his side. Very near to his master the Werewolf went, like any dog, and had no care to seek again the wood. When the King had brought him safely to his own castle, he rejoiced greatly, for the beast was fair and strong, no mightier had any man seen. Much pride had the King in his marvellous beast. He held him so dear, that he bade all those who wished for his love, to cross the Wolf in naught, neither to strike him with a rod, but ever to see that he was richly fed and kennelled warm. This commandment the Court observed willingly. So all the day the Wolf sported with the lords, and at night he lay within the chamber of the King. There was not a man who did not make much of the beast, so frank was he and debonair. None had reason to do him wrong, forever was he about his master, and for his part did evil to none. Every day were these two companions together, and all perceived that the King loved him as his friend.

Hearken now to that which chanced.

The King held a high Court, and bade his great vassals and barons, and all the lords of his venery to the feast. Never was there a goodlier feast, nor one set forth with sweeter show and pomp. Amongst those who were bidden, came that same knight who had the wife of Bisclavaret for dame. He came to the castle, richly gowned, with a fair company, but little he deemed whom he would find so near. Bisclavaret marked his foe the moment he stood within the hall. He ran towards him, and seized him with his fangs, in the King's very presence, and to the view of all. Doubtless he would have done him much mischief, had not the King called and chidden him, and threatened him with a rod. Once, and twice, again, the Wolf set upon the knight in the very light of day. All men marvelled at his malice, for sweet and serviceable was the beast, and to that hour had shown hatred of none. With one consent the household deemed that this deed was done with full reason, and that the Wolf had suffered at the knight's hand some bitter wrong. Right wary of his foe was the knight until the feast had ended, and all the barons had taken farewell of their lord, and departed, each to his own house. With these, amongst the very first, went that lord whom Bisclavaret so fiercely had assailed. Small was the wonder that he was glad to go.

No long while after this adventure it came to pass that the courteous King would hunt in that forest where Bisclavaret was found. With the prince came his wolf, and a fair company. Now at nightfall the King abode within a certain lodge of that country, and this was known of that dame who before was the wife of Bisclavaret. In the morning the lady clothed her in her most dainty apparel, and hastened to the lodge, since she desired to speak with the King, and to offer him a rich present. When the lady entered in the chamber, neither man nor leash might restrain the fury of the Wolf. He became as a mad dog in his hatred and malice. Breaking from his bonds he sprang at the lady's face, and bit the nose from her visage. From every side men ran to the succour of the dame. They beat off the wolf from his prey, and for a little would have cut him in pieces with their swords. But a certain wise counsellor said to the King,

"Sire, hearken now to me. This beast is always with you, and there is not one of us all who has not known him for long. He goes in and out amongst us, nor has molested any man, neither done wrong or felony to any, save only to this dame, one only time as we have seen. He has done evil to this lady, and to that knight, who is now the husband of the dame. Sire, she was once the wife of that lord who was so close and private to your heart, but who went, and none might find where he had gone. Now, therefore, put the dame in a sure place, and question her straitly, so that she may tell—if perchance she knows thereof—for what reason this Beast holds her in such mortal hate. For many a strange deed has chanced, as well we know, in this marvellous land of Brittany."

The King listened to these words, and deemed the counsel good. He laid hands upon the knight, and put the dame in surety in another place. He caused them to be questioned right straitly, so that their torment was very grievous. At the end, partly because of her distress, and partly by reason of her exceeding fear, the lady's lips were loosed, and she told her tale. She showed them of the betrayal of her lord, and how his raiment was stolen from the hollow stone. Since then she knew not where he went, nor what had befallen him, for he had never come again to his own land. Only, in her heart, well she deemed and was persuaded, that Bisclavaret was he.

Straightway the King demanded the vesture of his baron, whether this were to the wish of the lady, or whether it were against her wish. When the raiment was brought him, he caused it to be spread before Bisclavaret, but the Wolf made as though he had not seen. Then that cunning and crafty counsellor took the King apart, that he might give him a fresh rede.

"Sire," said he, "you do not wisely, nor well, to set this raiment before Bisclavaret, in the sight of all. In shame and much tribulation must he lay aside the beast, and again become man. Carry your wolf within your most secret chamber, and put his vestment therein. Then close the door upon him, and leave him alone for a space. So we shall see presently whether the ravening beast may indeed return to human shape."

The King carried the Wolf to his chamber, and shut the doors upon him fast. He delayed for a brief while, and taking two lords of his fellowship with him, came again to the room. Entering therein, all three, softly together, they found the knight sleeping in the King's bed, like a little child. The King ran swiftly to the bed and taking his friend in his arms, embraced and kissed him fondly, above a hundred times. When man's speech returned once more, he told him of his adventure. Then the King restored to his friend the fief that was stolen from him, and gave such rich gifts, moreover, as I cannot tell. As for the wife who had betrayed Bisclavaret, he bade her avoid his country, and chased her from the realm. So she went forth, she and her second lord together, to seek a more abiding city, and were no more seen.

The adventure that you have heard is no vain fable. Verily and indeed it chanced as I have said. The Lay of the Werewolf, truly, was written that it should ever be borne in mind.

THE LAY OF THE ASH TREE

Now will I tell you the Lay of the Ash Tree, according to the story that I know.

In ancient days there dwelt two knights in Brittany, who were neighbours and close friends. These two lords were brave and worthy gentlemen, rich in goods and lands, and near both in heart and home. Moreover each was wedded to a dame. One of these ladies was with child, and when her time was come, she was delivered of two boys. Her husband was right happy and content. For the joy that was his, he sent messages to his neighbour, telling that his wife had brought forth two sons, and praying that one of them might be christened with his name. The rich man was at meat when the messenger came before him. The servitor kneeled before the dais, and told his message in his ear. The lord thanked God for the happiness that had befallen his friend, and bestowed a fair horse on the bringer of good tidings. His wife, sitting at board with her husband, heard the story of the messenger, and smiled at his news. Proud she was, and sly, with an envious heart, and a rancorous tongue.

She made no effort to bridle her lips, but spoke lightly before the servants of the house, and said,

"I marvel greatly that so reputable a man as our neighbour, should publish his dishonour to my lord. It is a shameful thing for any wife to have two children at a birth. We all know that no woman brings forth two at one bearing, except two husbands have aided her therein."

Her husband looked upon her in silence for awhile, and when he spoke it was to blame her very sternly.

"Wife," he said, "be silent. It is better to be dumb, than to utter such words as these. As you know well, there is not a breath to tarnish this lady's good name."

The folk of the house, who listened to these words, stored them in their hearts, and told abroad the tale, spoken by their lady. Very soon it was known throughout Brittany. Greatly was the lady blamed for her evil tongue, and not a woman who heard thereof—whether she were rich or poor—but who scorned her for her malice. The servant who carried the message, on his return repeated to his lord of what he had seen and heard. Passing heavy was the knight, and knew not what to do. He doubted his own true wife, and suspected her the more sorely, because she had done naught that was in any way amiss.

The lady, who so foully slandered her fellow, fell with child in the same year. Her neighbour was avenged upon her, for when her term was come, she became the mother of two daughters. Sick at heart was she. She was right sorrowful, and lamented her evil case.

"Alas," she said, "what shall I do, for I am dishonoured for all my days. Shamed I am, it is the simple truth.

When my lord and his kinsfolk shall hear of what has chanced, they will never believe me a stainless wife. They will remember how I judged all women in my plight. They will recall how I said before my house, that my neighbour could not have been doubly a mother, unless she had first been doubly a wife. I have the best reason now to know that I was wrong, and I am caught in my own snare. She who digs a pit for another, cannot tell that she may not fall into the hole herself. If you wish to speak loudly concerning your neighbour, it is best to say nothing of him but in praise. The only way to keep me from shame, is that one of my children should die. It is a great sin; but I would rather trust to the mercy of God, than suffer scorn and reproach for the rest of my life."

The women about her comforted her as best they might in this trouble. They told her frankly that they would not suffer such wrong to be done, since the slaying of a child was not reckoned a jest. The lady had a maiden near her person, whom she had long held and nourished. The damsel was a freeman's daughter, and was greatly loved and cherished of her mistress. When she saw the lady's tears, and heard the bitterness of her complaint, anguish went to her heart, like a knife. She stooped over her lady, striving to bring her comfort.

"Lady," she said, "take it not so to heart. Give over this grief, for all will yet be well. You shall deliver me one of these children, and I will put her so far from you, that you shall never see her again, nor know shame because of her. I will carry her safe and sound to the door of a church. There I will lay her down. Some honest man shall find her, and—please God—will be at the cost of her nourishing."

Great joy had the lady to hear these words. She promised the maiden that in recompense of her service, she would grant her such guerdon as she should wish. The maiden took the babe—yet smiling in her sleep—and wrapped her in a linen cloth. Above this she set a piece of sanguine silk, brought by the husband of this dame from a bazaar in Constantinople—fairer was never seen. With a silken lace they bound a great ring to the child's arm. This ring was of fine gold, weighing fully an ounce, and was set with garnets most precious.

Letters were graven thereon, so that those who found the maid might understand that she came of a good house. The damsel took the child, and went out from the chamber. When night was come, and all was still, she left the town, and sought the high road leading through the forest. She held on her way, clasping the baby to her breast, till from afar, to her right hand, she heard the howling of dogs and the crowing of cocks. She deemed that she was near a town, and went the lighter for the hope, directing her steps, there, whence the noises came. Presently the damsel entered in a fair city, where was an Abbey, both great and rich. This Abbey was worshipfully ordered, with many nuns in their office and degree, and an Abbess in charge of all. The maiden gazed upon the mighty house, and considered its towers and walls, and the church with its belfry. She went swiftly to the door, and setting the child upon the ground, kneeled humbly to make her prayer.

"Lord," said she, "for the sake of Thy Holy Name, if such be Thy will, preserve this child from death."

Her petition ended, the maiden looked about her, and saw an ash tree, planted to give shadow in a sunny place. It was a fair tree, thick and leafy, and was divided into four strong branches. The maiden took the child again in her arms, and running to the ash, set her within the tree. There she left her, commending her to the care of God. So she returned to her mistress, and told her all that she had done.

Now in this Abbey was a porter, whose duty it was to open the doors of the church, before folk came to hear the service of God. This night he rose at his accustomed hour, lighted candles and lamps, rang the bells, and set wide the doors. His eyes fell upon the silken stuff within the ash. He thought at first that some bold thief had hidden his spoil within the tree. He felt with his hand to discover what it might be, and found that it was a little child. The porter praised God for His goodness; he took the babe, and going again to his house, called to his daughter, who was a widow, with an infant yet in the cradle.

"Daughter," he cried, "get from bed at once; light your candle, and kindle the fire. I bring you a little child, whom I have found within our ash. Take her to your breast; cherish her against the cold, and bathe her in warm water."

The widow did according to her father's will. She kindled a fire, and taking the babe, washed and cherished her in her need. Very certain she was, when she saw that rich stuff of crimson samite, and the golden ring about the arm, that the girl was come of an honourable race. The next day, when the office was ended, the porter prayed the Abbess that he might have speech with her as she left the church. He related his story, and told of the finding of the child. The Abbess bade him to fetch the child, dressed in such fashion as she was discovered in the ash. The porter returned to his house, and showed the babe right gladly to his dame. The Abbess observed the infant closely, and said that she would be at the cost of her nourishing, and would cherish her as a sister's child. She commanded the porter strictly to forget that he took her from the ash. In this manner it chanced that the maiden was tended of the Abbess. The lady considered the maid as her niece, and since she was taken from the ash, gave her the name of Frêne. By this name she was known of all, within the Abbey precincts, where she was nourished.

When Frêne came to that age in which a girl turns to woman, there was no fairer maiden in Brittany, nor so sweet a damsel. Frank, she was, and open, but discreet in semblance and in speech. To see her was to love her, and to prize her smile above the beauty of the world. Now at Dol there lived a lord of whom much good was spoken. I will tell you his name. The folk of his country called him Buron. This lord heard speak of the maiden, and began to love her, for the sweetness men told of her. As he rode home from some tournament, he passed near the convent, and prayed the Abbess that he might look upon her niece. The Abbess gave him his desire. Greatly was the maiden to his mind. Very fair he found her, sweetly schooled and fashioned, modest and courteous to all. If he might not win her to his love, he counted himself the more forlorn. This lord was at his wits end, for he knew not what to do. If he repaired often to the convent, the Abbess would consider of the cause of his comings, and he would never again see the maiden with his eyes. One thing only gave him a little hope. Should he endow the Abbey of his wealth, he would make it his debtor forever. In return he might ask a little room, where he might abide to have their fellowship, and, at times, withdraw him from the world. This he did. He gave richly of his goods to the Abbey. Often, in return, he went to the convent, but for other reasons than for penitence and peace. He besought the maiden, and with prayers and promises, persuaded her to set upon him her love. When this lord was assured that she loved him, on a certain day he reasoned with her in this manner.

"Fair friend," said he, "since you have given me your love, come with me, where I can cherish you before all the world. You know, as well as I, that if your aunt should perceive our friendship, she would be passing wrath, and grieve beyond measure. If my counsel seems good, let us flee together, you with me, and I with you. Certes, you shall never have cause to regret your trust, and of my riches you shall have the half."

When she who loved so fondly heard these words, she granted of her tenderness what it pleased him to have, and followed after where he would. Frêne fled to her lover's castle, carrying with her that silken cloth and ring, which might do her service on a day. These the Abbess had given her again, telling her how one morning at prime she was found upon an ash, this ring and samite her only wealth, since she was not her niece. Right carefully had Frêne guarded her treasure from that hour. She shut them closely in a little chest, and this coffret she bore with her in her flight, for she would neither lose them nor forget.

The lord, with whom the maiden fled, loved and cherished her very dearly. Of all the men and servants of his house, there was not one—either great or small—but who loved and honoured her for her simplicity. They lived long together in love and content, till the fair days passed, and trouble came upon this lord. The knights of his realm drew together, and many a time urged that he should put away his friend, and wed with some rich gentlewoman. They would be joyous if a son were born, to come after to his fief and heritage. The peril was too great to suffer that he remained a bachelor, and without an heir. Never more would they hold him as lord, or serve him with a good heart, if he would not do according to their will.

There being naught else to do, the lord deferred to this counsel of his knights, and begged them to name the lady whom he needs must wed.

"Sir," answered they, "there is a lord of these parts, privy to our counsel, who has but one child, a maid, his only heir. Broad lands will he give as her dowry. This damsel's name is Coudre, and in all this country there is none so fair. Be advised: throw away the ash rod you carry, and take the hazel as your staff.[1] The ash is a barren stock; but the hazel is thick with nuts and delight. We shall be content if you take this maiden as your wife, so it be to the will of God, and she be given you of her kinsfolk."

Buron demanded the hand of the lady in marriage, and her father and kin betrothed her to the lord. Alas! it was hid from all, that these two were twin sisters. It was Frêne's lot to be doubly abandoned, and to see her lover become her sister's husband. When she learned that her friend purposed taking to himself a wife, she made no outcry against his falseness. She continued to serve her lord faithfully, and was diligent in the business of his house. The sergeant and the varlet were marvellously wrathful, when they knew that she must go from amongst them. On the day appointed for the marriage, Buron bade his friends and acquaintance to the feast. Together with these came the Archbishop, and those of Dol who held of him their lands. His betrothed was brought to his home by her mother. Great dread had the mother because of Frêne, for she knew of the love that the lord bore the maiden, and feared lest her daughter should be a stranger in her own hall. She spoke to her son-in-law, counselling him to send Frêne from his house, and to find her an honest man for her husband. Thus there would be quittance between them. Very splendid was the feast. Whilst all was mirth and jollity, the damsel visited the chambers, to see that each was ordered to her lord's pleasure. She hid the torment in her heart, and seemed neither troubled nor downcast. She compassed the bride with every fair observance, and waited upon her right daintily.

Her courage was marvellous to that company of lords and ladies, who observed her curiously. The mother of the bride regarded her also, and praised her privily. She said aloud that had she known the sweetness of this lady, she would not have taken her lover from her, nor spoiled her life for the sake of the bride. The night being come the damsel entered in the bridal chamber to deck the bed against her lord. She put off her mantle, and calling the chamberlains, showed them how their master loved to lie. His bed being softly arrayed, a coverlet was spread upon the linen sheets. Frêne looked upon the coverlet: in her eyes it showed too mean a garnishing for so fair a lord. She turned it over in her mind, and going to her coffret she took therefrom that rich stuff of sanguine silk, and set it on the couch. This she did not only in honour of her friend, but that the Archbishop might not despise the house, when he blessed the marriage bed, according to the rite. When all was ready the mother carried the bride to that chamber where she should lie, to disarray her for the night. Looking upon the bed she marked the silken coverlet, for she had never seen so rich a cloth, save only that in which she wrapped her child. When she remembered of this thing, her heart turned to water. She summoned a chamberlain.

"Tell me," she said, "tell me in good faith where this garniture was found."

"Lady," he made reply, "that you shall know. Our damsel spread it on the bed, because this dossal is richer than the coverlet that was there before."

The lady called for the damsel. Frêne came before her in haste, being yet without her mantle. All the mother moved within her, as she plied her with questions.

"Fair friend, hide it not a whit from me. Tell me truly where this fair samite was found; whence came it; who gave it to you? Answer swiftly, and tell me who bestowed on you this cloth?"

The damsel made answer to her:

"Lady, my aunt, the Abbess, gave me this silken stuff, and charged me to keep it carefully. At the same time she gave me a ring, which those who put me forth, had bound upon me."

"Fair friend, may I see this ring?"

"Certes, lady, I shall be pleased to show it."

The lady looked closely on the ring, when it was brought. She knew again her own, and the crimson samite flung upon the bed. No doubt was in her mind. She knew and was persuaded that Frêne was her very child. All words were spoken, and there was nothing more to hide.

"Thou art my daughter, fair friend."

Then for reason of the pity that was hers, she fell to the ground, and lay in a swoon. When the lady came again to herself, she sent for her husband, who, all adread, hastened to the chamber. He marvelled the more sorely when his wife fell at his feet, and embracing him closely, entreated pardon for the evil that she had done.

Knowing nothing of her trespass, he made reply, "Wife, what is this? Between you and me there is nothing to call for forgiveness. Pardon you may have for whatever fault you please. Tell me plainly what is your wish."

"Husband, my offence is so black, that you had better give me absolution before I tell you the sin. A long time ago, by reason of lightness and malice, I spoke evil of my neighbour, whenas she bore two sons at a birth. I fell afterwards into the very pit that I had digged. Though I told you that I was delivered of a daughter, the truth is that I had borne two maids. One of these I wrapped in our stuff of samite, together with the ring you gave me the first time we met, and caused her to be laid beside a church. Such a sin will out. The cloth and the ring I have found, and I have recognised our maid, whom I had lost by my own folly. She is this very damsel—so fair and amiable to all—whom the knight so greatly loved. Now we have married the lord to her sister."

The husband made answer, "Wife, if your sin be double, our joy is manifold. Very tenderly hath God dealt with us, in giving us back our child. I am altogether joyous and content to have two daughters for one. Daughter, come to your father's side."

The damsel rejoiced greatly to hear this story. Her father tarried no longer, but seeking his son-in-law, brought him to the Archbishop, and related the adventure. The knight knew such joy as was never yet. The Archbishop gave counsel that on the morrow he would part him and her whom he had joined together. This was done, for in the morning he severed them, bed and board. Afterwards he married Frêne to her friend, and her father accorded the damsel with a right good heart. Her mother and sister were with her at the wedding, and for dowry her father gave her the half of his heritage. When they returned to their own realm they took Coudre, their daughter, with them. There she was granted to a lord of those parts, and rich was the feast.

When this adventure was bruited abroad, and all the story, the Lay of the Ash Tree was written, so called of the lady, named Frêne.

The Lay of the Honeysuckle

With a glad heart and right good mind will I tell the Lay that men call Honeysuckle; and that the truth may be known of all it shall be told as many a minstrel has sung it to my ear, and as the scribe hath written it for our delight. It is of Tristan and Isoude, the Queen. It is of a love which passed all other love, of love from whence came wondrous sorrow, and whereof they died together in the selfsame day.

King Mark was sorely wrath with Tristan, his sister's son, and bade him avoid his realm, by reason of the love he bore the Queen. So Tristan repaired to his own land, and dwelt for a full year in South Wales, where he was born. Then since he might not come where he would be, Tristan took no heed to his ways, but let his life run waste to Death. Marvel not overmuch thereat, for he who loves beyond measure must ever be sick in heart and hope, when he may not win according to his wish. So sick in heart and mind was Tristan that he left his kingdom, and returned straight to the realm of his banishment, because that in Cornwall dwelt the Queen. There he hid privily in the deep forest, withdrawn from the eyes of men; only when the evening was come, and all things sought their rest, he prayed the peasant and other mean folk of that country, of their charity to grant him shelter for the night. From the serf he gathered tidings of the King. These gave again to him what they, in turn, had taken from some outlawed knight. Thus Tristan learned that when Pentecost was come King Mark purposed to hold high Court at Tintagel, and keep the feast with pomp and revelry; moreover that thither would ride Isoude, the Queen.

When Tristan heard this thing he rejoiced greatly, since the Queen might not adventure through the forest, except he saw her with his eyes. After the King had gone his way, Tristan entered within the wood, and sought the path by which the Queen must come. There he cut a wand from out a certain hazel-tree, and having trimmed and peeled it of its bark, with his dagger he carved his name upon the wood. This he placed upon her road, for well he knew that should the Queen but mark his name she would bethink her of her friend. Thus had it chanced before. For this was the sum of the writing set upon the wand, for Queen Isoude's heart alone: how that in this wild place Tristan had lurked and waited long, so that he might look upon her face, since without her he was already dead. Was it not with them as with the Honeysuckle and the Hazel tree she was passing by! So sweetly laced and taken were they in one close embrace, that thus they might remain whilst life endured. But should rough hands part so fond a clasping, the hazel would wither at the root, and the honeysuckle must fail. Fair friend, thus is the case with us, nor you without me, nor I without you.

Now the Queen fared at adventure down the forest path. She spied the hazel wand set upon her road, and well she remembered the letters and the name. She bade the knights of her company to draw rein, and dismount from their palfreys, so that they might refresh themselves a little. When her commandment was done she withdrew from them a space, and called to her Brangwaine, her maiden, and own familiar friend. Then she hastened within the wood, to come on him whom more she loved than any living soul. How great the joy between these twain, that once more they might speak together softly, face to face. Isoude showed him her delight. She showed in what fashion she strove to bring peace and concord betwixt Tristan and the King, and how grievously his banishment had weighed upon her heart. Thus sped the hour, till it was time for them to part; but when these lovers freed them from the other's arms, the tears were wet upon their cheeks. So Tristan returned to Wales, his own realm, even as his uncle bade. But for the joy that he had had of her, his friend, for her sweet face, and for the tender words that she had spoken, yea, and for that writing upon the wand, to remember all these things, Tristan, that cunning harper, wrought a new Lay, as shortly I have told you. Goatleaf, men call this song in English. Chèvrefeuille it is named in French; but Goatleaf or Honeysuckle, here you have the very truth in the Lay that I have spoken.

THE LAY OF EQUITAN

In ancient days many a noble lord lived in Brittany beyond the Seas. By reason of their courtesy and nobleness they would gladly keep in remembrance the deeds that were done in the land. That these marvellous things should not be forgotten they fashioned them into Lays. Amongst these Lays I have heard tell of one which is not made to die as though it had never been.

Equitan, lord of Nantes, was a loyal and courteous gentleman, of great worth, beloved by all in his own country. He was set on pleasure, and was Love's lover, as became a gentle knight. Like many others who dote on woman, he observed neither sense nor measure in love. But it is in the very nature of Love that proportion cannot enter into the matter.

Equitan had for seneschal a right brave and loyal knight, who was captain of his army, and did justice in his realm. He was often abroad upon his master's business, for the King would not forego his delight for any reason whatever. To dance, to hunt, to fish within the river—this was all his joy. This seneschal was married to a wife, by whom great evil came upon the land. Very desirable was the lady; passing tender of body, and sweet of vesture, coiffed and fretted with gold. Her eyes were blue; her face warmly coloured, with a fragrant mouth, and a dainty nose. Certainly she had no peer in all the realm. The King had heard much in praise of this lady and many a time saluted her upon the way. He had also sent her divers gifts. Often he considered in his mind how best he might get speech with the dame. For his privy pleasure this amorous King went to chase in that country where the seneschal had his castle. The lady being in her own house, Equitan craved a lodging for the night. By this means when the hunt was done, he could speak with her, and show what was in his heart. Equitan found the lady as discreet as courteous. He looked closely upon her, for she was fair of face and person, and sweet of semblance and address. Love bound him captive to his car. The god loosed a shaft which entered deeply in his breast. The arrow pierced to his heart, and from thenceforth he cared nothing for measure, or kingship, or delight. Equitan was so surprised of the lady, that he remained silent and pensive. He heard nothing, and nothing he could do. All night he lay in unrest upon the bed, reproaching himself for what had come to pass.

"Alas," said he, "what evil fate has led me into this land! The sight only of this lady has put such anguish into my heart that my members fail beneath me. It is Love, I deem, who rides me thus cruelly. But if I love this lady I shall do a great wrong. She is the wife of my seneschal, and it is my duty to keep the same love and faith to him as I would wish him to observe with me. If by any means I could know what is in her mind, I should be the easier, for torment is doubled that you bear alone. There is not a dame, however curst, but would rather love than not; for if she were a contemner of love where would be her courtesy? But if she loves, there is not a woman under the sky who would not suck thereout all the advantage that she may. If the matter came to the ears of the seneschal, he ought not to think too hardly of me. He cannot hope to keep such treasure for himself alone; and, certes, I shall claim my portion."

Equitan tossed on his bed, and sighed. His thoughts were still on the lady, so that in a little he said, "I think of the ford, before I come to the river. I go too quickly, for I know not yet whether the lady will take me as her friend. But know I will as swiftly as I can, since I cannot get rest or sleep. I will come before her as soon as it is day, and if she feels as I feel, the sooner I shall be rid of my pain."

The King kept vigil till the daylight came at last. He arose and went forth, as if to the chase. He returned presently, telling that he was sick, and going straight to his chamber, lay upon his bed. The seneschal was very troubled, for he could not imagine the sickness of which his master felt the pangs. He counselled his wife to seek their guest, that she might cheer and comfort him in his trouble. When they were alone the King opened to her his heart. He told her that he was dying for her love, and that if she had no more than friendship to offer, he preferred death before life.

"Sire," replied the dame, "I require a little time to think of what you say, for I cannot answer yes or no, without thought, in a business of this moment. I am not of your wealth, and you are too high a lord, for your love to do more than rest lightly on me. When you have had your desire, it will as lightly fly away. My sorrow would be overlong, if I should love you, and grant you what you wish. It is much the best that between you and me love should not be spoken of. You are a puissant prince; my husband is one of your vassals, and faith and trust should bind us—not the dangerous bond of love. Love is only lasting between like and like. Better is the love of an honest man—so he be of sense and worth—than that of a prince or king, with no loyalty in him. She who sets her love more highly than she can reach, may pluck no fruit from the tree. The rich man deems that love is his of right. He prays little of his friend, for he thinks none dare take her from his hand, and that her tenderness is his by prize of lordship."

When she had ceased, Equitan made answer, "Lady, I can offer you but short thanks for your words, since they savour of scant courtesy. You speak of love as a burgess makes a bargain. Those who desire to get, rather than to give, often find that they have the worser half of the business. There is no lady under heaven—so she be courteous and kind and of a good heart—but would grant her grace to a true lover, even though she have beneath her cloak only a rich prince in his castle. Those who care but for a fresh face—tricksters in love as a cozener with dice—are justly flouted and deceived, as oftentimes we see. None wastes pity on him who receives the stripes he deserves. Dear lady, let me make myself plain. Do not regard me as your King; look on me as your servant and your friend. I give my word and plight my troth that all my happiness shall be found in your pleasure. Let me not die for your love. You shall be the Dame, and I the page; you shall be the scornful beauty, and I the prayer at your knee."

The King prayed the lady so urgently, so tenderly he sued for grace, that at the last she assured him of her love, and gave him the gift of her heart. They granted rings one to another, and pledged affiance between them. They kept this faith, and guarded this love, till they died together, and there was an end to all.

Equitan and the lady loved for a great while without it coming to the ears of any. When the King desired to have speech of his friend, he told his household that he would be alone, since it was the day appointed for his bleeding. The King having shut the doors of his chamber, there was none so bold as to enter therein, save he were bidden of his lord. Whilst he was busied in this fashion, the seneschal sat in open court to hear the pleas and right the wrong. He was as much to the King's mind, as his wife was to the King's heart. The lord was so assotted upon the lady that he would neither take to himself a wife, nor listen to a word upon the matter. His people blamed him loudly, so loudly that it came to the ears of the lady. She was passing heavy, for she feared greatly that the barons would have their way. When next she had speech with Equitan, in place of the kiss and sweetness of her customary greeting, she came before him making great sorrow and in tears. The King inquiring the reason of her dolour, the lady replied, "Sire, I lament our love, and the trouble I always said would be mine. You are about to wed the daughter of some King, and my good days are over. Everybody says so, and I know it to be true. What will become of me when you put me away! I will die, rather than lose you, for I may have no other comfort."

The King made answer very tenderly, "Fair friend, you need not fear. There will never be wife of mine to put you from me. I shall never wed, except your husband die, and then it is you who would be my queen and lady. I will leave you for no other dame."

The lady thanked him sweetly for his words. Much was she beholden to him in her heart. Since she was assured that he would not leave her for any other, she turned over swiftly in her mind the profit that would come from her husband's death. Much happiness might be bought at a little cost, if Equitan would lend his aid.

The King made answer that he would do her will to the utmost of his power, whether her counsel were for good or evil.

"Sire," said the lady, "let it please you to hunt the forest within the country where I dwell. You can lodge in my lord's castle, and there you must be bled. Three days after your surgery is done, you must call for your bath. My lord shall be bled with you, so that he may go to his bathing at the same time. It will be your part to keep him at your side, and make him your constant companion. It will be mine to heat the water, and to carry the baths to your chamber. My husband's bath shall boil so fiercely, that no breathing man, having entered therein, may come forth living. When he is dead you must call for your people, and show them how the seneschal has died suddenly in his bath."

Because of his love the King granted her desire, and promised to do according to her will. Before three months were done the King rode to the chase within the lady's realm. He caused surgeons to bleed him for his health, and the seneschal with him. He said that he would take his bath on the third day, and the seneschal required his, too, to be made ready. The lady caused the water to be heated, and carried the baths to the chamber. According to her device she set a bath beside each bed, filling with boiling water that bath which her lord should enter. Her lord had gone forth for a little, so for a space the King and the lady were alone. They sat on the husband's bed, and looked tenderly each on the other, near by that heated bath. The door of the chamber was kept by a young damsel to give them warning. The seneschal made haste to return, and would have struck on the door of the chamber, but was stayed by the maiden. He put her by, and in his impatience flung the door wide open. Entering he found his master and his wife clasped in each other's arms. When the King saw the seneschal he had no thought but to hide his dishonour. He started up, and sprang with joined feet in the bath that was filled with boiling water. There he perished miserably, in the very snare he had spread for another, who was safe and sound. The seneschal marked what had happened to the King. In his rage he turned to his wife, and laying hands upon her thrust her, head first, in the selfsame bath. So they died together, the King first, and the lady afterwards, with him.

Those who are willing to listen to fair words, may learn from this ensample, that he who seeks another's ill often brings the evil upon himself.

As I have told you before, of this adventure the Bretons made the Lay of Equitan, the lady whom he loved, and of their end.

THE LAY OF MILON

He who would tell divers tales must know how to vary the tune. To win the favour of any, he must speak to the understanding of all. I purpose in this place to show you the story of Milon, and—since few words are best—I will set out the adventure as briefly as I may.

Milon was born in South Wales. So great was his prowess that from the day he was dubbed knight there was no champion who could stand before him in the lists. He was a passing fair knight, open and brave, courteous to his friends, and stern to his foes. Men praised his name in whatever realm they talked of gallant deeds—Ireland, Norway, and Wales, yea, from Jutland even to Albania. Since he was praised by the frank, he was therefore envied of the mean. Nevertheless, by reason of his skill with the spear, he was counted a very worshipful knight, and was honourably entreated by many a prince in divers lands.

In Milon's own realm there lived a lord whose name has gone from mind. With this baron dwelt his daughter, a passing fair and gracious damsel. Much talk had this maiden heard of Milon's knightly deeds, so that she began to set her thoughts upon him, because of the good men spoke of him. She sent him a message by a sure hand, saying that if her love was to his mind, sweetly would it be to her heart. Milon rejoiced greatly when he knew this thing. He thanked the lady for her words, giving her love again in return for her own, and swearing that he would never depart therefrom any day of his days. Beyond this courteous answer Milon bestowed on the messenger costly gifts, and made him promises that were richer still.

"Friend," said he, "of your charity I pray you that I may have speech with my friend, in such a fashion that none shall know of our meeting. Carry her this, my golden ring. Tell her, on my part, that so she pleases she shall come to me, or, if it be her better pleasure, I will go to her."

The messenger bade farewell, and returned to his lady. He placed the ring in her hand, saying that he had done her will, as he was bidden to do.

Right joyous was the damsel to know that Milon's love was tender as her own. She required her friend to come for speech within the private garden of her house, where she was wont to take her delight. Milon came at her commandment. He came so often, and so dearly she loved him, that in the end she gave him all that maid may give. When the damsel perceived how it was with her, she sent messages to her friend, telling him of her case, and making great sorrow.

"I have lost my father and all his wealth," said the lady, "for when he hears of this matter he will make of me an example. Either I shall be tormented with the sword, or else he will sell me as a slave in a far country."

(For such was the usage of our fathers in the days of this tale).

Milon grieved sorely, and made answer that he would do the thing the damsel thought most seemly to be done.

"When the child is born," replied the lady, "you must carry him forthwith to my sister. She is a rich dame, pitiful and good, and is wedded to a lord of Northumberland. You will send messages with the babe—both in writing and by speech—that the little innocent is her sister's child. Whether it be a boy or girl his mother will have suffered much because of him, and for her sister's sake you will pray her to cherish the babe. Beyond this I shall set your signet by a lace about his neck, and write letters wherein shall be made plain the name of his sire, and the sad story of his mother. When he shall have grown tall, and of an age to understand these matters, his aunt will give him your ring, and rehearse to him the letter. If this be done, perchance the orphan will not be fatherless all his days."

Milon approved the counsel of the lady, and when her time had come she was brought to bed of a boy. The old nurse who tended her mistress was privy to the damsel's inmost mind. So warily she went to work, so cunning was she in gloss and concealment, that none within the palace knew that there was aught to hide. The damsel looked upon her boy, and saw that he was very fair. She laced the ring about his neck, and set the letter that it were death to find, within a silken chatelaine. The child was then placed in his cradle, swathed close in white linen. A pillow of feathers was put beneath his head, and over all was laid a warm coverlet, wadded with fur. In this fashion the ancient nurse gave the babe to his father, who awaited him within the garden. Milon commended the child to his men, charging them to carry him loyally, by such towns as they knew, to that lady beyond the Humber. The servitors set forth, bearing the infant with them. Seven times a day they reposed them in their journey, so that the women might nourish the babe, and bathe and tend him duly. They served their lord so faithfully, keeping such watch upon the way, that at the last they won to the lady to whom they were bidden. The lady received them courteously, as became her breeding. She broke the seal of the letter, and when she was assured of what was therein, marvellously she cherished the infant. These having bestowed the boy in accordance with their lord's commandment, returned to their own land.

Milon went forth from his realm to serve beyond the seas for guerdon. His friend remained within her house and was granted by her father in marriage to a right rich baron of that country. Though this baron was a worthy knight, justly esteemed of all his fellows, the damsel was grieved beyond measure when she knew her father's will. She called to mind the past, and regretted that Milon had gone from the country, since he would have helped her in her need.

"Alas!" said the lady, "what shall I do? I doubt that I am lost, for my lord will find that his bride is not a maid. If this becomes known they will make me a bondwoman for all my days. Would that my friend were here to free me from this coil. It were good for me to die rather than to live, but by no means can I escape from their hands. They have set warders about me, men, old and young, whom they call my chamberlains, contemners of love, who delight themselves in sadness. But endure it I must, for, alas, I know not how to die."

So on the appointed day the lady was wedded to the baron, and her husband took her to dwell with him in his fief.

When Milon returned to his own country he was right heavy and sorrowful to learn of this marriage. He lamented his wretched case, but in this he found comfort, that he was not far from the realm where the lady abode whom so tenderly he loved. Milon commenced to think within himself how best he might send letters to the damsel that he was come again to his home, yet so that none should have knowledge thereof. He wrote a letter, and sealed it with his seal. This message he made fast to the neck, and hid within the plumage of a swan that was long his, and was greatly to his heart. He bade his squire to come, and made him his messenger.

"Change thy raiment swiftly," said he, "and hasten to the castle of my friend. Take with thee my swan, and see that none, neither servant nor handmaid, delivers the bird to my lady, save thyself alone."

The squire did according to his lord's commandment. He made him ready quickly, and went forth, bearing the swan with him. He went by the nearest road, and passing through the streets of the city, came before the portal of the castle. In answer to his summons the porter drew near.

"Friend," said he, "hearken to me. I am of Caerleon, and a fowler by craft. Within my nets I have snared the most marvellous swan in the world. This wondrous bird

I would bestow forthwith upon your lady, but perforce I must offer her the gift with my own hand."

"Friend," replied the porter, "fowlers are not always welcomed of ladies. If you come with me I will bring you where I may know whether it pleases my lady to have speech with you and to receive your gift."

The porter entered in the hall, where he found none but two lords seated at a great table, playing chess for their delight. He swiftly returned on his steps, and the fowler with him, so furtively withal that the lords were not disturbed at their game, nor perceived aught of the matter. They went therefore to the chamber of the lady. In answer to their call the door was opened to them by a maiden, who led them before her dame. When the swan was proffered to the lady it pleased her to receive the gift. She summoned a varlet of her household and gave the bird to his charge, commanding him to keep it safely, and to see that it ate enough and to spare.

"Lady," said the servitor, "I will do your bidding. We shall never receive from any fowler on earth such another bird as this. The swan is fit to serve at a royal table, for the bird is plump as he is fair."

The varlet put the swan in his lady's hands. She took the bird kindly, and smoothing his head and neck, felt the letter that was hidden beneath its feathers. The blood pricked in her veins, for well she knew that the writing was sent her by her friend. She caused the fowler to be given of her bounty, and bade the men to go forth from her chamber. When they had parted the lady called a maiden to her aid. She broke the seal, and unfastening the letter, came upon the name of Milon at the head. She kissed the name a hundred times through her tears.

When she might read the writing she learned of the great pain and dolour that her lover suffered by day and by night. In you—he wrote—is all my pleasure, and in your white hands it lies to heal me or to slay. Strive to find a plan by which we may speak as friend to friend, if you would have me live. The knight prayed her in his letter to send him an answer by means of the swan. If the bird were well guarded, and kept without provand for three days, he would of a surety fly back to the place from whence he came, with any message that the lady might lace about his neck.

When the damsel had considered the writing, and understood what was put therein, she commanded that her bird should be tended carefully, and given plenteously to eat and to drink. She held him for a month within her chamber, but this was less from choice, than for the craft that was necessary to obtain the ink and parchment requisite for her writing. At the end she wrote a letter according to her heart, and sealed it with her ring. The lady caused the swan to fast for three full days; then having concealed the message about his neck, let him take his flight. The bird was all anhungered for food, and remembering well the home from which he drew, he returned thither as quickly as his wings might bear him.

He knew again his town, and his master's house, and descended to the ground at Milon's very feet. Milon rejoiced greatly when he marked his own. He caught the bird by his wings, and crying for his steward, bade him give the swan to eat. The knight removed the missive from the messenger's neck. He glanced from head to head of the letter, seeking the means that he hoped to find, and the salutation he so tenderly wished. Sweet to his heart was the writing, for the lady wrote that without him there was no joy in her life, and since it was his desire to hear by the swan, it would be her pleasure also.

For twenty years the swan was made the messenger of these two lovers, who might never win together. There was no speech between them, save that carried by the bird. They caused the swan to fast for three days, and then sent him on his errand. He to whom the letter came, saw to it that the messenger was fed to heart's desire. Many a time the swan went upon his journey, for however strictly the lady was held of her husband, there was none who had suspicion of a bird.

The dame beyond the Humber nourished and tended the boy committed to her charge with the greatest care. When he was come to a fitting age she made him to be knighted of her lord, for goodly and serviceable was the lad. On the same day the aunt read over to him the letter, and put in his hand the ring. She told him the name of his mother, and his father's story. In all the world there was no worthier knight, nor a more chivalrous and gallant gentleman. The lad hearkened diligently to the lady's tale. He rejoiced greatly to hear of his father's prowess, and was proud beyond measure of his renown. He considered within himself, saying to his own heart, that much should be required of his father's son, and that he would not be worthy of his blood if he did not endeavour to merit his name. He determined therefore that he would leave his country, and seek adventure as a knight errant, beyond the sea. The varlet delayed no longer than the evening. On the morrow he bade farewell to his aunt, who having warned and admonished him for his good, gave him largely of her wealth, to bring him on his way. He rode to Southampton, that he might find a ship equipped for sea, and so came to Barfleur. Without any tarrying the lad went straight to Brittany, where he spent his money and himself in feasts and in tourneys. The rich men of the land were glad of his friendship, for there was none who bore himself better in the press with spear or with sword. What he took from the rich he bestowed on such knights as were poor and luckless. These loved him greatly, since he gained largely and spent freely, granting of his wealth to all. Wherever this knight sojourned in the realm he bore away the prize. So debonair was he and chivalrous that his fame and praise crossed the water, and were noised abroad in his own land. Folk told how a certain knight from beyond the Humber, who had passed the sea in quest of wealth and honour, had so done, that by reason of his prowess, his liberality, and his modesty, men called him the Knight Peerless, since they did not know his name.

This praise of the good knight, and of his deeds, came to be heard of Milon. Very dolent was he and sorely troubled that so young a knight should be esteemed above his fathers. He marvelled greatly that the stout spears of the past had not put on their harness and broken a lance for their ancient honour. One thing he determined, that he would cross the sea without delay, so that he might joust with the dansellon, and abate his pride. In wrath and anger he purposed to fight, to beat his adversary from the saddle, and bring him at last to shame. After this was ended he would seek his son, of whom he had heard nothing, since he had gone from his aunt's castle. Milon caused his friend to know of his wishes. He opened out to her all his thought, and craved her permission to depart. This letter he sent by the swan, commending the bird to her care.

When the lady heard of her lover's purpose, she thanked him for his courtesy, for greatly was his counsel to her mind. She approved his desire to quit the realm for the sake of his honour, and far from putting let and hindrance in his path, trusted that in the end he would bring again her son. Since Milon was assured of his friend's goodwill, he arrayed himself richly, and crossing the sea to Normandy, came afterwards into the land of the Bretons. There he sought the friendship of the lords of that realm, and fared to all the tournaments of which he might hear. Milon bore himself proudly, and gave graciously of his wealth, as though he were receiving a gift. He sojourned till the winter was past in that land, he, and a brave company of knights whom he held in his house with him. When Easter had come, and the season that men give to tourneys and wars and the righting of their private wrongs, Milon considered how he could meet with the knight whom men called Peerless. At that time a tournament was proclaimed to be held at Mont St. Michel. Many a Norman and Breton rode to the game; knights of Flanders and of France were there in plenty, but few fared from England. Milon drew to the lists amongst the first. He inquired diligently of the young champion, and all men were ready to tell from whence he came, and of his harness, and of the blazon on his shield. At length the knight appeared in the lists and Milon looked upon the adversary he so greatly desired to see. Now in this tournament a knight could joust with that lord who was set over against him, or he could seek to break a lance with his chosen foe. A player must gain or lose, and he might find himself opposed either by his comrade or his enemy. Milon did well and worshipfully in the press, and was praised of many that day. But the Knight Peerless carried the cry from all his fellows, for none might stand before him, nor rival him in skill and address. Milon observed him curiously. The lad struck so heavily, he thrust home so shrewdly, that Milon's hatred changed to envy as he watched. Very comely showed the varlet, and much to Milon's mind. The older knight set himself over against the champion, and they met together in the centre of the field. Milon struck his adversary so fiercely, that the lance splintered in his gauntlet; but the young knight kept his seat without even losing a stirrup. In return his spear was aimed with such cunning that he bore his antagonist to the ground. Milon lay upon the earth bareheaded, for his helmet was unlaced in the shock. His hair and beard showed white to all, and the varlet was heavy to look on him whom he had overthrown. He caught the destrier by the bridle, and led him before the stricken man.

"Sir," said he, "I pray you to get upon your horse. I am right grieved and vexed that I should have done this wrong. Believe me that it was wrought unwittingly."

Milon sprang upon his steed. He approved the courtesy of his adversary, and looking upon the hand that held his bridle, he knew again his ring. He made inquiry of the lad.

"Friend," said he, "hearken to me. Tell me now the name of thy sire. How art thou called; who is thy mother? I have seen much, and gone to and fro about the world. All my life I have journeyed from realm to realm, by reason of tourneys and quarrels and princes' wars, yet never once by any knight have I been borne from my horse. This day I am overthrown by a boy, and yet I cannot help but love thee."

The varlet answered, "I know little of my father. I understand that his name is Milon, and that he was a knight of Wales. He loved the daughter of a rich man, and was loved again. My mother bore me in secret, and caused me to be carried to Northumberland, where I was taught and tended. An old aunt was at the costs of my nourishing. She kept me at her side, till of all her gifts she gave me horse and arms, and sent me here, where I have remained. In hope and wish I purpose to cross the sea, and return to my own realm. There I would seek out my father, and learn how it stands between him and my mother. I will show him my golden ring, and I will tell him of such privy matters that he may not deny our kinship, but must love me as a son, and ever hold me dear."

When Milon heard these words he could endure them no further. He got him swiftly from his horse, and taking the lad by the fringe of his hauberk, he cried, "Praise be to God, for now am I healed. Fair friend, by my faith thou art my very son, for whom I came forth from my own land, and have sought through all this realm."

The varlet climbed from the saddle, and stood upon his feet. Father and son kissed each other tenderly, with many comfortable words. Their love was fair to see, and those who looked upon their meeting, wept for joy and pity.

Milon and his son departed from the tournament so soon as it came to an end, for the knight desired greatly to speak to the varlet at leisure, and to open before him all his mind. They rode to their hostel, and with the knights of their fellowship, passed the hours in mirth and revelry. Milon spoke to the lad of his mother. He told him of their long love, and how she was given by her father in marriage to a baron of his realm. He rehearsed the years of separation, accepted by both with a good heart, and of the messenger who carried letters between them, when there was none they dared to trust in, save only the swan.

The son made answer,

"In faith, fair father, let us return to our own land. There I will slay this husband, and you shall yet be my mother's lord."

This being accorded between them, on the morrow they made them ready for the journey, and bidding farewell to their friends, set forth for Wales. They embarked in a propitious hour, for a fair wind carried the ship right swiftly to its haven. They had not ridden far upon their road, when they met a certain squire of the lady's household on his way to Brittany, bearing letters to Milon. His task was done long before sundown in chancing on the knight. He gave over the sealed writing with which he was charged, praying the knight to hasten to his friend without any tarrying, since her husband was in his grave. Milon rejoiced greatly when he knew this thing. He showed the message to his son, and pressed forward without pause or rest. They made such speed, that at the end they came to the castle where the lady had her lodging. Light of heart was she when she clasped again her child. These two fond lovers sought neither countenance of their kin, nor counsel of any man. Their son handselled them together, and gave the mother to his sire. From the day they were wed they dwelt in wealth and in sweetness to the end of their lives.

Of their love and content the minstrel wrought this Lay. I, also, who have set it down in writing, have won guerdon enough just by telling over the tale.

THE LAY OF YONEC

Since I have commenced I would not leave any of these Lays untold. The stories that I know I would tell you forthwith. My hope is now to rehearse to you the story of Yonec, the son of Eudemarec, his mother's first born child.

In days of yore there lived in Britain a rich man, old and full of years, who was lord of the town and realm of Chepstow. This town is builded on the banks of the Douglas, and is renowned by reason of many ancient sorrows which have there befallen. When he was well stricken in years this lord took to himself a wife, that he might have children to come after him in his goodly heritage. The damsel, who was bestowed on this wealthy lord, came of an honourable house, and was kind and courteous, and passing fair. She was beloved by all because of her beauty, and none was more sweetly spoken of from Chepstow to Lincoln, yea, or from there to Ireland. Great was their sin who married the maiden to this aged man. Since she was young and gay, he shut her fast within his tower, that he might the easier keep her to himself. He set in charge of the damsel his elder sister, a widow, to hold her more surely in ward. These two ladies dwelt alone in the tower, together with their women, in a chamber by themselves. There the damsel might have speech of none, except at the bidding of the ancient dame. More than seven years passed in this fashion. The lady had no children for her solace, and she never went forth from the castle to greet her kinsfolk and her friends. Her husband's jealousy was such that when she sought her bed, no chamberlain or usher was permitted in her chamber to light the candles. The lady became passing heavy. She spent her days in sighs and tears. Her loveliness began to fail, for she gave no thought to her person. Indeed at times she hated the very shadow of that beauty which had spoiled all her life.

Now when April had come with the gladness of the birds, this lord rose early on a day to take his pleasure in the woods. He bade his sister to rise from her bed to make the doors fast behind him. She did his will, and going apart, commenced to read the psalter that she carried in her hand. The lady awoke, and shamed the brightness of the sun with her tears. She saw that the old woman was gone forth from the chamber, so she made her complaint without fear of being overheard.

"Alas," said she, "in an ill hour was I born. My lot is hard to be shut in this tower, never to go out till I am carried to my grave. Of whom is this jealous lord fearful that he holds me so fast in prison? Great is a man's folly always to have it in mind that he may be deceived. I cannot go to church, nor hearken to the service of God. If I might talk to folk, or have a little pleasure in my life, I should show the more tenderness to my husband, as is my wish. Very greatly are my parents and my kin to blame for giving me to this jealous old man, and making us one flesh. I cannot even look to become a widow, for he will never die. In place of the waters of baptism, certainly he was plunged in the flood of the Styx. His nerves are like iron, and his veins quick with blood as those of a young man. Often have I heard that in years gone by things chanced to the sad, which brought their sorrows to an end. A knight would meet with a maiden, fresh and fair to his desire. Damsels took to themselves lovers, discreet and brave, and were blamed of none. Moreover since these ladies were not seen of any, except their friends, who was there to count them blameworthy! Perchance I deceive myself, and in spite of all the tales, such adventures happened to none. Ah, if only the mighty God would but shape the world to my wish!"

When the lady had made her plaint, as you have known, the shadow of a great bird darkened the narrow window, so that she marvelled what it might mean. This falcon flew straightway into the chamber, jessed and hooded from the glove, and came where the dame was seated. Whilst the lady yet wondered upon him, the tercel became a young and comely knight before her eyes. The lady marvelled exceedingly at this sorcery. Her blood turned to water within her, and because of her dread she hid her face in her hands. By reason of his courtesy the knight first sought to persuade her to put away her fears.

"Lady," said he, "be not so fearful. To you this hawk shall be as gentle as a dove. If you will listen to my words I will strive to make plain what may now be dark.

I have come in this shape to your tower that I may pray you of your tenderness to make of me your friend. I have loved you for long, and in my heart have esteemed your love above anything in the world. Save for you I have never desired wife or maid, and I shall find no other woman desirable, until I die. I should have sought you before, but I might not come, nor even leave my own realm, till you called me in your need. Lady, in charity, take me as your friend."

The lady took heart and courage whilst she hearkened to these words. Presently she uncovered her face, and made answer. She said that perchance she would be willing to give him again his hope, if only she had assurance of his faith in God. This she said because of her fear, but in her heart she loved him already by reason of his great beauty. Never in her life had she beheld so goodly a youth, nor a knight more fair.

"Lady," he replied, "you ask rightly. For nothing that man can give would I have you doubt my faith and affiance. I believe truly in God, the Maker of all, who redeemed us from the woe brought on us by our father Adam, in the eating of that bitter fruit. This God is and was and ever shall be the life and light of us poor sinful men. If you still give no credence to my word, ask for your chaplain; tell him that since you are sick you greatly desire to hear the Service appointed by God to heal the sinner of his wound. I will take your semblance, and receive the Body of the Lord. You will thus be certified of my faith, and never have reason to mistrust me more."

When the sister of that ancient lord returned from her prayers to the chamber, she found that the lady was awake. She told her that since it was time to get her from bed, she would make ready her vesture. The lady made answer that she was sick, and begged her to warn the chaplain, for greatly she feared that she might die. The agèd dame replied,

"You must endure as best you may, for my lord has gone to the woods, and none will enter in the tower, save me."

Right distressed was the lady to hear these words. She called a woman's wiles to her aid, and made seeming to swoon upon her bed. This was seen by the sister of her lord, and much was she dismayed. She set wide the doors of the chamber, and summoned the priest. The chaplain came as quickly as he was able, carrying with him the Lord's Body. The knight received the Gift, and drank of the Wine of that chalice; then the priest went his way, and the old woman made fast the door behind him.

The knight and the lady were greatly at their ease; a comelier and a blither pair were never seen. They had much to tell one to the other, but the hours passed till it was time for the knight to go again to his own realm. He prayed the dame to give him leave to depart, and she sweetly granted his prayer, yet so only that he promised to return often to her side.

"Lady," he made answer, "so you please to require me at any hour, you may be sure that I shall hasten at your pleasure. But I beg you to observe such measure in the matter, that none may do us wrong. This old woman will spy upon us night and day, and if she observes our friendship, will certainly show it to her lord. Should this evil come upon us, for both it means separation, and for me, most surely, death."

The knight returned to his realm, leaving behind him the happiest lady in the land. On the morrow she rose sound and well, and went lightly through the week. She took such heed to her person, that her former beauty came to her again. The tower that she was wont to hate as her prison, became to her now as a pleasant lodging, that she would not leave for any abode and garden on earth. There she could see her friend at will, when once her lord had gone forth from the chamber. Early and late, at morn and eve, the lovers met together. God grant her joy was long, against the evil day that came.

The husband of the lady presently took notice of the change in his wife's fashion and person. He was troubled in his soul, and misdoubting his sister, took her apart to reason with her on a day. He told her of his wonder that his dame arrayed her so sweetly, and inquired what this should mean. The crone answered that she knew no more than he, "for we have very little speech one with another. She sees neither kin nor friend; but, now, she seems quite content to remain alone in her chamber."

The husband made reply,

"Doubtless she is content, and well content. But by my faith, we must do all we may to discover the cause. Hearken to me. Some morning when I have risen from bed, and you have shut the doors upon me, make pretence to go forth, and let her think herself alone. You must hide yourself in a privy place, where you can both hear and see. We shall then learn the secret of this new found joy."

Having devised this snare the twain went their ways. Alas, for those who were innocent of their counsel, and whose feet would soon be tangled in the net.

Three days after, this husband pretended to go forth from his house. He told his wife that the King had bidden him by letters to his Court, but that he should return speedily. He went from the chamber, making fast the door. His sister arose from her bed, and hid behind her curtains, where she might see and hear what so greedily she desired to know. The lady could not sleep, so fervently she wished for her friend. The knight came at her call, but he might not tarry, nor cherish her more than one single hour. Great was the joy between them, both in word and tenderness, till he could no longer stay. All this the crone saw with her eyes, and stored in her heart. She watched the fashion in which he came, and the guise in which he went. But she was altogether fearful and amazed that so goodly a knight should wear the semblance of a hawk. When the husband returned to his house—for he was near at hand—his sister told him that of which she was the witness, and of the truth concerning the knight. Right heavy was he and wrathful. Straightway he contrived a cunning gin for the slaying of this bird. He caused four blades of steel to be fashioned, with point and edge sharper than the keenest razor. These he fastened firmly together, and set them securely within that window, by which the tercel would come to his lady. Ah, God, that a knight so fair might not see nor hear of this wrong, and that there should be none to show him of such treason.

On the morrow the husband arose very early, at daybreak, saying that he should hunt within the wood.

His sister made the doors fast behind him, and returned to her bed to sleep, because it was yet but dawn. The lady lay awake, considering of the knight whom she loved so loyally. Tenderly she called him to her side. Without any long tarrying the bird came flying at her will. He flew in at the open window, and was entangled amongst the blades of steel. One blade pierced his body so deeply, that the red blood gushed from the wound. When the falcon knew that his hurt was to death, he forced himself to pass the barrier, and coming before his lady fell upon her bed, so that the sheets were dabbled with his blood. The lady looked upon her friend and his wound, and was altogether anguished and distraught.

"Sweet friend," said the knight, "it is for you that my life is lost. Did I not speak truly that if our loves were known, very surely I should be slain?"

On hearing these words the lady's head fell upon the pillow, and for a space she lay as she were dead. The knight cherished her sweetly. He prayed her not to sorrow overmuch, since she should bear a son who would be her exceeding comfort. His name should be called Yonec. He would prove a valiant knight, and would avenge both her and him by slaying their enemy. The knight could stay no longer, for he was bleeding to death from his hurt. In great dolour of mind and body he flew from the chamber. The lady pursued the bird with many shrill cries. In her desire to follow him she sprang forth from the window. Marvellous it was that she was not killed outright, for the window was fully twenty feet from the ground. When the lady made her perilous leap she was clad only in her shift. Dressed in this fashion she set herself to follow the knight by the drops of blood which dripped from his wound. She went along the road that he had gone before, till she lighted on a little lodge. This lodge had but one door, and it was stained with blood. By the marks on the lintel she knew that Eudemarec had refreshed him in the hut, but she could not tell whether he was yet within. The damsel entered in the lodge, but all was dark, and since she might not find him, she came forth, and pursued her way. She went so far that at the last the lady came to a very fair meadow. She followed the track of blood across this meadow, till she saw a city near at hand. This fair city was altogether shut in with high walls. There was no house, nor hall, nor tower, but shone bright as silver, so rich were the folk who dwelt therein. Before the town lay a still water. To the right spread a leafy wood, and on the left hand, near by the keep, ran a clear river. By this broad stream the ships drew to their anchorage, for there were above three hundred lying in the haven. The lady entered in the city by the postern gate. The gouts of freshly fallen blood led her through the streets to the castle. None challenged her entrance to the city; none asked of her business in the streets; she passed neither man nor woman upon her way. Spots of red blood lay on the staircase of the palace. The lady entered and found herself within a low ceiled room, where a knight was sleeping on a pallet. She looked upon his face and passed beyond. She came within a larger room, empty, save for one lonely couch, and for the knight who slept thereon. But when the lady entered in the third chamber she saw a stately bed, that well she knew to be her friend's. This bed was of inwrought gold, and was spread with silken cloths beyond price. The furniture was worth the ransom of a city, and waxen torches in sconces of silver lighted the chamber, burning night and day. Swiftly as the lady had come she knew again her friend, directly she saw him with her eyes. She hastened to the bed, and incontinently swooned for grief. The knight clasped her in his arms, bewailing his wretched lot, but when she came to her mind, he comforted her as sweetly as he might.

"Fair friend, for God's love I pray you get from hence as quickly as you are able. My time will end before the day, and my household, in their wrath, may do you a mischief if you are found in the castle. They are persuaded that by reason of your love I have come to my death. Fair friend, I am right heavy and sorrowful because of you."

The lady made answer, "Friend, the best thing that can befall me is that we shall die together. How may I return to my husband? If he finds me again he will certainly slay me with the sword."

The knight consoled her as he could. He bestowed a ring upon his friend, teaching her that so long as she wore the gift, her husband would think of none of these things, nor care for her person, nor seek to revenge him for his wrongs. Then he took his sword and rendered it to the lady, conjuring her by their great love, never to give it to the hand of any, till their son should be counted a brave and worthy knight. When that time was come she and her lord would go—together with the son—to a feast. They would lodge in an Abbey, where should be seen a very fair tomb. There her son must be told of this death; there he must be girt with this sword. In that place shall be rehearsed the tale of his birth, and his father, and all this bitter wrong. And then shall be seen what he will do.

When the knight had shown his friend all that was in his heart, he gave her a bliaut, passing rich, that she might clothe her body, and get her from the palace. She went her way, according to his command, bearing with her the ring, and the sword that was her most precious treasure. She had not gone half a mile beyond the gate of the city when she heard the clash of bells, and the cries of men who lamented the death of their lord. Her grief was such that she fell four separate times upon the road, and four times she came from out her swoon. She bent her steps to the lodge where her friend had refreshed him, and rested for awhile. Passing beyond she came at last to her own land, and returned to her husband's tower. There, for many a day, she dwelt in peace, since—as Eudemarec foretold—her lord gave no thought to her outgoings, nor wished to avenge him, neither spied upon her any more.

In due time the lady was delivered of a son, whom she named Yonec. Very sweetly nurtured was the lad. In all the realm there was not his like for beauty and generosity, nor one more skilled with the spear. When he was of a fitting age the King dubbed him knight. Hearken now, what chanced to them all, that selfsame year.

It was the custom of that country to keep the feast of St. Aaron with great pomp at Caerleon, and many another town besides. The husband rode with his friends to observe the festival, as was his wont. Together with him went his wife and her son, richly apparelled. As the roads were not known of the company, and they feared to lose their way, they took with them a certain youth to lead them in the straight path. The varlet brought them to a town; in all the world was none so fair. Within this city was a mighty Abbey, filled with monks in their holy habit. The varlet craved a lodging for the night, and the pilgrims were welcomed gladly of the monks, who gave them meat and drink near by the Abbot's table. On the morrow, after Mass, they would have gone their way, but the Abbot prayed them to tarry for a little, since he would show them his chapter house and dormitory, and all the offices of the Abbey. As the Abbot had sheltered them so courteously, the husband did according to his wish.

Immediately that the dinner had come to an end, the pilgrims rose from table, and visited the offices of the Abbey. Coming to the chapter house they entered therein, and found a fair tomb, exceeding great, covered with a silken cloth, banded with orfreys of gold. Twenty torches of wax stood around this rich tomb, at the head, the foot, and the sides. The candlesticks were of fine gold, and the censer swung in that chantry was fashioned from an amethyst. When the pilgrims saw the great reverence vouchsafed to this tomb, they inquired of the guardians as to whom it should belong, and of the lord who lay therein. The monks commenced to weep, and told with tears, that in that place was laid the body of the best, the bravest, and the fairest knight who ever was, or ever should be born. "In his life he was King of this realm, and never was there so worshipful a lord. He was slain at Caerwent for the love of a lady of those parts. Since then the country is without a King. Many a day have we waited for the son of these luckless lovers to come to our land, even as our lord commanded us to do."

When the lady heard these words she cried to her son with a loud voice before them all.

"Fair son," said she, "you have heard why God has brought us to this place. It is your father who lies dead within this tomb. Foully was he slain by this ancient Judas at your side."

With these words she plucked out the sword, and tendered him the glaive that she had guarded for so long a season. As swiftly as she might she told the tale of how Eudemarec came to have speech with his friend in the guise of a hawk; how the bird was betrayed to his death by the jealousy of her lord; and of Yonec the falcon's son. At the end she fell senseless across the tomb, neither did she speak any further word until the soul had gone from her body. When the son saw that his mother lay dead upon her lover's grave, he raised his father's sword and smote the head of that ancient traitor from his shoulders. In that hour he avenged his father's death, and with the same blow gave quittance for the wrongs of his mother. As soon as these tidings were published abroad, the folk of that city came together, and setting the body of that fair lady within a coffin, sealed it fast, and with due rite and worship placed it beside the body of her friend. May God grant them pardon and peace. As to Yonec, their son, the people acclaimed him for their lord, as he departed from the church.

Those who knew the truth of this piteous adventure, after many days shaped it to a Lay, that all men might learn the plaint and the dolour that these two friends suffered by reason of their love.

ENDNOTES

1. This is a play on words; *Frêne* in the French, meaning ash, and *Coudre* meaning hazel. ↵